Romancing the Lakes of Minnesota ~Christmas~

Lanna Farrell
Diane Wiggert
Rhonna Krueger
Kristy Johnson
Kathleen Nordstrom
Rose Marie Meuwissen
Peg Pierson
Ann Nardone

Published by

nordic
PUBLISHING

Nordic Publishing, LLC.
P. O. Box 923, Prior Lake, MN. 55372
www.NordicPublishing.biz

ISBN: 1539731820
ISBN-13: 978-1539731825

ACKNOWLEDGEMENTS

We would like to offer a special thanks to published authors for Beta Reads and the Minnesota Lakes Anthology Committee. Also for the services provided in publishing this anthology, we would like to thank our editor, Leanore Elliott and Paula Miller for formatting this book.

ROMANCING THE LAKES OF MINNESOTA
~CHRISTMAS~

1. **A Song to Remember** by *Lanna Farrell*

Lake Minnetonka

Mack MacKenzie, head of security for Crystal Angel, the famous pop singer caught his angel in his arms as she fell from exhaustion into unconsciousness. Waking in the hospital, Crystal saw Mack, her one and only true love of her life waiting for her. She'd already fallen in love with him, it was time to make him hers.

2. **Best Laid Plans** by *Diane Wiggert*

Carl's Lake

Evan Hovland has a plan for everything including Christmas, but when his girlfriend, Maya, refuses his proposal even best laid plans can crumble. Can he win her back before the holidays? It's time to make a new plan.

3. **Christmas Joy** by *Rhonna Krueger*

Lake Minnetonka

NY Times Best Seller, Joy Abraham, has come home to put her mentor, father and the greatest man she'd ever known into a care facility. Now, she has come face to face with Pete Anderson, driver, maintenance and caretaker of her family home. For as long as Joy could remember, she'd had a crush on the man. Can she make everything work out for the best and maybe have her happily ever after?

4. **Mistletoe Miracle** by *Kristy Johnson*

Lake Andrusia

Mistletoe has long been the center of much folklore. It has been said to have mystical powers promoting love and healing. Combined with the miracle of Christmas, Jenna Otherday and her parents embark on a journey of rediscovering lost love and forgiveness.

5. **Naughty and Nice** by *Kathleen Nordstrom*

Crystal Lake

Yes, Franny and Chloe there is a Santa Claus. He knows when you've been naughty, but won't forget when you've been nice. Some Christmas wishes require a little help from Santa's elves to make them come true.

6. **Old Yule Log Fires** by *Rose Marie Meuwissen*

Lake Minnetonka

The Old Log theater manager, Tara, has a Christmas crisis. Ty, her high school sweetheart, now a Hollywood heartthrob, is back and starring in the big holiday show. It's been ten years. Sparks will fly, but can the smoldering ashes from an old log catch fire and allow the flames of true love to burn once again?

7. **The Elf** by *Peg Pierson*

Hatch Lake

Wildlife biologist, Chrissy, doesn't believe in holiday miracles. But when Eirnik the Elf literally crashes into her life, with a dazzling smile and one of Santa's reindeer, the scientist may have to believe in the magic of Christmas.

8. **The Last Customer on Christmas Eve** by *Ann Nardone*

Lake Winnibigoshish

Can a lover from the past and her last customer for the evening at the Aurora Boulais Cabin Resort's bar and grille, make this Lisa's best Christmas Eve ever, or will the cold of his betrayal keep her heart frozen?

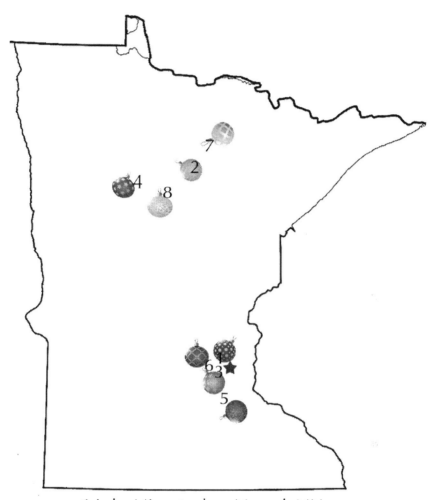

1 Lake Minnetonka - Mound, MN
2 Carl's Lake - Spring Lake, MN
3 Lake Minnetonka - Wayzata, MN
4 Lake Andrusia - Bemidji, MN
5 Crystal Lake - Burnsville, MN
6 Lake Minnetonka - Excelsior, MN
7 Hatch Lake - Bigfork, MN
8 Lake Winnibigoshish - Bena, MN

A SONG TO REMEMBER
Lanna Farrell

Lake Minnetonka - Mound, MN

Crystal Angel sang "Joy to the World" at the Excel Center, located in downtown St. Paul. The streets around the center were beautifully decorated and Christmas was in full swing. She hated the holidays because it reminded her she had no one. She also hated the fact her manager pushed her to pretend to like the holidays. All the festivities had forced her to be so busy, and she wasn't getting the needed rest she craved.

It was a sold out show and there were nearly 20,000 people here. Though, with the bright lights shining in her face, it was nearly impossible to see them. Her head began to throb with the flashing lights and the pounding of the music. Another migraine.

Crystal actually hated Christmas. No family, not many friends and even though people surrounded her every day for the past two years, she still felt lonely and alone.

Crystal sung the last song into the microphone for her fans. The great stadium echoed the music and with her vision blurring, she signaled to her manager, a wave, then two fingers held up, he nodded. She needed to end the concert. She felt exhausted and had finished the entire play list she'd arranged for tonight. She shouted into the mic, "Thank you all for coming. Happy holidays." She waved and handed the mic to someone, just didn't know or care who.

The crowd went crazy and cheered. The lights dimmed and she could see out into the audience, everyone stood on their feet.

She waved quickly then rushed to the back. She didn't want to be sick and cause embarrassment while vomiting on stage.

Over the last several years, she'd become one of the biggest pop singers to hit the charts and move to the top. She knew she'd over done it. Her body suffered and didn't even have enough time to enjoy the career she'd originally started. She couldn't tell if it was the writing or singing the songs. Dear Lord, thank you for helping me through the trials and errors tonight's performance brought. She spoke to God as if he were a friend. Tonight had been different on stage. God was in the house. She could feel him as she sang. He carried her through the concert. With her strong faith, she had felt the electricity and emotion. She'd been able to pour out her soul and open her heart to the love she had for God. Her belief had kept her faith strong, even when her childhood and into her teens were spent in the foster care system, she knew God loved her. Her true feelings poured out to the audience through every song. If not for Him, she knew she wouldn't have made it through this performance.

A Christmas concert for her hometown, repaying her Minnesota fans, would always be the place she chose to honor during this time of the year. She felt proud she was able to finish. Suddenly, there were pains shooting through her head and she felt her body sway slightly. She swiftly steadied herself by leaning on a large speaker, waved once more, then headed to the back. Her four-inch stilettos seemed to be taller as her head spun and she almost lost her balance, again. She knew now, it was time for a much needed rest of at least a few months. Her next tour didn't start until way into March of the next year.

After she reached the back stage area, the dizziness became so severe, her mind was spinning. Right before the darkness took hold—she collapsed and heard his soft whisper, "I got you, love." Strong arms wrapped around her and she knew she was safe.

***

Mack, short for Mackenzie, Walker, caught Crystal, his little angel, in his strong arms as she collapsed. He'd argued earlier with her and told her he didn't feel right letting her out there, on the stage, which was hot and stifling from all the equipment and lights. Why didn't she listen to him? She fought for every single day. Today though, she'd not said more than a few words to anyone, so he knew she'd been really sick. Now, he knew for sure and they were heading straight to the ER.

Speaking into the mic attached to his ear he ordered the crew, "Get that ambulance and where the hell is the doctor?"

"Mack, easy, they're here. You're good." Frank Tyson nodded.

Mack looked toward the delicate package in his arms. "Sorry, Frankie, I'm just so frustrated. She's in a bad way."

"Yeah, I know. Move your ass." Frankie yelled back into his ear.

"She's light as a feather. I don't think she's eaten in weeks." Mack knew his anger and disappointment fueled his attitude towards the team of people who kept her safe. He'd fallen in love with her during high school. She'd made it clear to everyone, her career was important and she had to remain focused.

Returning home from an eight-year stint in the military, he'd followed along with her success. During the time he fought the war overseas, her music kept him alive or the darkness would have suffocated him. Coming back scarred but matured, definitely changed him and trying to become a civilian was difficult and almost impossible sometimes.

The next time he saw her was at his father's funeral. He'd asked her out a few times and fallen head-over-heels in love with her. Then once again, her career pulled her out of his life.

He'd been surprised when she called him and asked him to lead her security team. Well, damn it! He sure hadn't done his job with her! He stared down at the little bundle in his arms with regrets he hadn't pursued her as he intended.

Picking up the pace, he jogged his way outside to the waiting vehicle. His booted feet hit the steps and he cleared his body through the doors, ending up inside. He laid her down on the gurney, sitting on the bench he grabbed her hand, and seat next to her ordered, "Go!"

The EMT in the back asked. "Sir, are you a relative?"

"I am head of security and that's all you need to know."

The driver looked in the back at him and nodded.

Mack hung on as the vehicle lurched forward.

Needing to touch her, he brushed the hair away from her face. They put in an IV, took her stats then put an oxygen mask on her. The Paramedic continued to take her blood pressure then held her arm for a pulse. His anger stirred at the other man touching her but it was a necessity. He felt confused about the strong emotions pumping through his mind.

He needed control. "What can you tell me?"

"Her oxygen levels are low," the young male EMT explained. "Sir, is there anything you can tell me about her?" The EMT was trying to do his job.

At the same time, Mack had his to do. He shook his head. After all, he knew nothing about what was going on with the woman he'd fallen in love with. She'd stayed to herself and not spoken to him much lately.

"Well, it's clear she's more than a client? Are you Mackenzie Walker?"

He nodded. "Yeah."

"The news and the tabloids have you blasted all over as her lover."

"I wish," he mumbled.

"She's dehydrated and the amount of fluids I'm pumping into her should bring her around pretty quickly." The EMT continued entering info into his little screen. Setting the tablet aside, he checked the IV, took all her vitals again, then glanced at him. "She's pretty sick. I can tell you that. She's probably worn out, fever, chills, and burning up. Has she been sick recently?"

Mack scrubbed his face. "I honestly don't know. She's a private person."

Crystal moaned a little. He gripped her hand. "W-what—?" she moaned.

He gripped her hand a little tighter. Leaning over by her, he asked, "I can't hear you, sweetie."

"What happened?" she whispered loud enough for him to hear

this time.

The male EMT leaned towards her and asked, "Ma'am, what is your name?"

"Crystalline Marie Anderson."

Mack, still feeling stunned, squeezed her hand. "Angel baby, you okay?" She hadn't told anyone her real legal name since probably high school, why now?

"Do you remember what happened?" The EMT asked.

"No," she mumbled.

Mack worried about her, more so than before. Did she have something else going on? She'd been working harder than usual. A three-month break meant no work for her and she hated the breaks. He knew that much about her. He despised them as well because he went from seeing her every day, to not at all.

They arrived at the hospital. He now figured she'd just pushed herself too far do this final concert for her hometown for the holidays.

***

Crystal couldn't remember what happened after feeling sick during her performance. All she knew was Mack had caught her as she passed out. She was thankful for the trust they had between them. She loved that man more than life. But she'd ruined her chances with him years ago.

Not sure how to put their broken relationship back together again, she had stopped trying and took what she could. His security team was the best for her and she'd been thankful for him in that regard.

Thankfully, every day she had him in her life. She'd been in love with that infuriating man but knew there was no way to be with him romantically, ever. She'd kept her love a secret to herself and didn't approach him again. Succeeding in keeping those unwanted thoughts from jumbling her mind and ruin their friendship.

When she woke up in a moving vehicle and heard the sirens, she knew exactly where she was—an ambulance. Her anxiety went through the rough and she panicked until she felt his strong callused hand squeeze hers. She opened her eyes slightly and looked over at his worried expression. His lips pinched and forward creased, she whispered, "I messed up, didn't I?"

He'd leaned his head down enough to hear her. "Yeah, baby doll. You wore yourself out to nothing," he whispered, tucking her hair behind her ear.

"No, I don't think I'm sick?" She tried to tear the mask off her face.

He frowned. "Stop, leave that alone. You need the extra oxygen.

She shook her head. "No, I want to talk." Crystal wished she could wash off the stage makeup, it felt fake and tight. She could barely manage a smile. She shouted loud enough for him to hear her this time. "I know I need to be checked out at the hospital. I'm not going to fight you on this one, Mack. My head is killing me and it feels like my chest is heavy and my lungs and throat hurt. I hardly have any strength left. I know this last concert made it worse." Closing her eyes she asked, "Will you pray with me, please?"

He nodded.

Her voice came out stronger, "Lord, please give me the strength to heal quickly and help the doctors find what is ailing me. God bless my friends and family during this season, Amen." She smiled weakly toward Mack, then whispered, "Thank you."

Crystal knew she hadn't served God enough quite yet. Not afraid of death, it was something she accepted a long time ago. She'd grown up in the foster system, so nothing surprised her.

They arrived at the hospital and when the EMTs unloaded her she insisted, "I need to hang onto Mack's hand, please?"

The EMT nodded. "Thank you." She looked up at her savior.

Mack smiled gently.

She closed her eyes to try and breathe deeply. She'd suffered from motion sickness since she was a kid and this wasn't helping.

Mack now walked next to the gurney.

She'd refrained from opening her eyes and causing more nausea, which was kicking her butt.

They put her in a triage room. "Mack, please come in with me. Don't leave me alone?" She begged.

He nodded. "Never, love."

She felt selfish and knew he loved her enough not to leave her alone, but being in love was a whole different emotion she held in secret not wanting to burden him with her crazy life.

She knew Mack suffered a painful past from his time spent in the military. She never asked about it because she thought it would be rude. When he felt ready, she was certain he would tell her about it.

Since he was the head of her security team, he literally seemed to be with her every second of her day and night. His square face, short black hair, and tanned skin made him handsome. He'd told her of his mixed genetic makeup. He had all different sorts of nationalities in him. Together, they were a good or even better than most couples. They just didn't have the intimate portion of the relationship. She craved to have that. His body alone woke hers and she craved him.

Mack leaned over. "What are you smiling about?"

Her face heated and she knew she blushed, mumbling, "Nothing. Don't know what you're talking about."

A nurse came in. "I'm sorry, sir, but you'll need to step out."

Mack nodded, leaned over and kissed her forehead. "Love you, babe. Listen to the doctors. I'll come in later."

When Mack walked out the door, she nodded. Her heart clenched and the back of her eyes burned from the tears she forced to stay in. Why did it feel as if she was losing her man? Her man? How embarrassing, she muttered, "Ugh."

"Excuse me?" The female nurse asked.

Crystal peered up and read her nametag. "Kelly? I'm sorry, mumbling to myself, bad habit." She fisted and tapped her chest.

The nurse made a few adjustments to the IV and bedding after taking her vitals she commented, "By the way, he's really a good looking guy."

"Yeah, he sure is." Crystal nodded. She knew they were only a few hours from her hometown where she'd planned to stay for a few months after this concert. Most likely, the concert tonight would be her final performance, which is why she'd put her entire soul into it.

"Are you two married?"

"Why do you ask that? I'm sure you know I'm not married." Crystal frowned. Weirded out that the nurse assumed something she knew nothing at all about.

"Well, I'm sorry if I offended you. I just thought…" The nurse stopped talking when the door opened as a man walked in wearing a white coat, she assumed was a doctor.

"Miss Crystal, you don't mind if I call you by your first name?"

She nodded. "Sure. Why is everyone walking around on egg shells around me?" Something made her feel angry but what, she didn't know. The doctor, nurse, even Mack. "Doctor, I need to figure out why I'm sick then I need to get home in time for Christmas." She felt as if she was whining, so she apologized, "I'm sorry that was rude of me."

The doctor chuckled. "Well, first off, I'm Doctor Richard Anderson. Miss Angel it's an honor to be able to care for you while you're here."

The nurse choked then coughed. She tried to stop, but after a few failed attempts to control the spell, she whispered, "Excuse me. I need to go get a drink of water." Coughing more, the nurse ran from the room.

"Gosh, I hope she's okay?" Crystal asked the doctor.

"She'll be fine. Back to you, young lady. We need to examine and figure out why you're in my ER. By the way, I'm the head physician. I wanted to take care of you myself."

"Don't give me any special attention." Crystal hated the fact everyone seemed to know her and she didn't want that.

After the doctor got done with his exam and ordered some tests, he shook her hand. "It's a pleasure and honor, Ms. Angel. My family loves your Christmas album. We listen to it every Christmas morning."

She smiled. "Thank you. I'm blessed to have fans such as yourself. Thank you doctor."

***

Mack hated the fact he was powerless to help Crystal and craved to stay by her side as the doctor poked and prodded her. When the doctor stepped out of her room, his booted feet rushed towards him. "Doctor? Do you mind talking to me?"

"Sure, come in here if you don't mind. I do know you two share something special." The doctor led him to the patient waiting area. The room being empty was a relief to Mack.

They shook hands and the doctor said, "It's a good thing she came in. Her body is weak and something has happened that caused trauma to her head. Did she fall or hit something?"

Mack shook his head. "I honestly don't know."

"Well, I'm running some tests to cover all areas and be on the safe side. If you two can think of anything that happened or if she was around someone who was sick, let me know."

"Okay, doc. Thanks." He walked away from the shorter man and back to Crystal's room. He immediately pulled down his poker face, which was always tough around her, he used his professional persona and he knew she hated it. Holding his body tight, straight, almost stiff with his hands behind his back, he asked, "How are you?"

"Mack, really? Sit your ass down. I need you to be my friend." Her eyes glossed and she seemed like she was about to cry. She still hadn't.

"What's wrong?" he asked, sitting down next to her.

"I just want to know what is wrong with me. Nobody seems to have any answers and I want to go home."

"I'm sorry. They're trying to do their best and figure all this out. It won't be long now. Hey, though, the doc seemed kind?" He pulled up the chair closer and took her hand into his. "What did he have to say?"

"He wasn't sure what could be causing all this other than I'm worn out. But I'm scared."

"Why? They said you were dehydrated, maybe that's all there is to it and with all those fluids, you'll start feeling well. Also, I've known you don't eat right. Trying to maintain your thin frame for show business. You're wearing yourself out. The others, your band, management, even the bus driver complained to me that you've been bitchy and no one wants to listen to it any longer. What's going on?"

"I don't know. But right now, I'm worried about the press having a field day." She reached out to him. "Hold my hand, please."

When he touched her cold and clammy palm, he knew instantly there was more to this than what she was saying. She was really sick.

He frowned. "What the hell is going on with you?"

***

Crystal looked up a few hours later when another doctor walked in. "Good day to you, young lady." He seemed like a happy, portly, short man who smiled, but there was something strange about him…like the smile didn't quite reach his eyes. She couldn't be sure but this man looked sad.

Mack had stayed by her side the entire time. She knew she'd fallen asleep on and off for the few hours she'd been here at this unfamiliar hospital in downtown St. Paul. Her sleep constantly disturbed with doctors, nurses and technicians coming in to do more tests and take blood. Oh, and vitals of course, each time they were normal, but all she wanted was to rest.

She didn't want anyone else to touch or exam her. She wanted to just go back to sleep. Grumbling she asked, "Can't this wait? I'm tired and want to sleep."

The doctor shook his head and laughed too loud, hurting her already sensitive and pounding head. "Nope, sorry."

Crystal opened her eyes slowly and nodded. "Fine. Then give it to me straight. No more BS, doc."

"Well, I'll have to say you're a lucky young woman. Number one on the list of wrongs, and that's from your blood draw, is you're dehydrated and malnourished, so I imagine you've completely worn yourself out but that's not all. Your platelets and iron are extremely low. That explains you fainting into this young man's arms, here." He pointed to Mack.

Crystal groaned as she tried to move her body and readjusted to sit up. Instead, she hit the upward button on her bed. She loved the fact Mack sat next to her, holding her hand. She didn't want his sympathy, she wanted his love. To take her home and please her as a man would a woman. Get your mind out of the gutter! She scolded herself.

Her entire body ached and she felt like she'd gotten run over by a truck. Knowing she'd done this entirely to herself. Her fans have always come before her health. Dang it! All she'd wanted was to do the concert and get her butt home. This weekend she was headed home to take a much-needed couple of months off. Dang it, her Christmas, ruined.

"Can I check you over quickly?" the doctor asked her permission kindly.

She nodded and opened her eyes just a tad. Immediately, the bright light of his exam light caused spots and a near migraine.

When she flinched, Mack stood up and growled out the words, "Enough, doc! Leave her alone."

"No, I need to finish the exam or I can't help her."

Crystal suddenly felt amused. She giggled slightly, causing the pain to shoot once again to her head. She grabbed her temples and tried to hold in the pain and relieve some of it.

She knew she'd better behave or she would have a migraine for sure. Matter of fact, she'd already given herself one with misbehaving. It was funny though, how the short, heavier set doctor standing up to tall, muscular, built like a brick building, Mack.

After the doctor left, Crystal's mood changed for the better and she let Mack hang onto her hand, it felt nice. She turned to him. "How long have I been sleeping?"

He turned his wrist and looked at his watch. "About five hours or so."

"You staying with me or leaving soon?" She knew once he got her sorry butt home, he would take off for his home in Texas. She felt sure he would want to spend it with his family.

"Until we walk out that door together, I'm staying." He pointed to the door, smiled and shook his head.

She dozed off for a bit again, then another man walked into her room and her eyes followed him until he stood next to the bed in blue scrubs. "Well, doctor, hope you have answers for me?"

Two of Mack's security men followed the guy in. "Mack, he said he's from the lab to take blood. Haven't they taken enough from her?"

"Hey, it's cool. The doctor needs a few more tests." Mack nodded towards the door.

The two men didn't need any other prompting, so they left immediately.

Mack looked up at the burly guy. "Being a nurse is quite the career apparently, to bring a big guy like you in."

"What do you mean?" the burly guy asked.

"Never mind. Just you surprised me being so big."

Crystal peered up at him. This nurse was bald, good looking, square faced, and wore a deadpan expression.

He swiftly poked, prodded and finally got enough blood from her for testing.

"They say I'm short on iron and he's taking more." She tried bringing a little laughter into the room. The two men were way too serious.

Neither of the men responded to her comment.

"Geez, you two need to lighten up a bit. It's almost Christmas."

The technician gazed at her and shook his head. "Sorry ma'am, I don't celebrate the holiday; I'm Jewish."

Crystal was speechless and felt an inch high.

Out of nowhere, Mack grabbed her hand and gave it a gentle squeeze. He smiled as he leaned over and kissed her right on the mouth.

Wow, now this was a moment she would never forget.

***

An hour or two passed as more of the hospital staff came and went before a new doctor finally walked back into room.

Mack was at the end of his rope. Sitting next to her as she slept, he faced the fact he'd fallen in love with her and he'd gotten tired of waiting. He needed to give her a choice, a career and him being a part of that or he was done and would walk away from all of it.

The doctor woke her once again, and started another exam. He flashed lights in her eyes again, then pushed and prodded at her head and neck.

Mack felt ready to beat the pulp out of the man.

The doctor let out an irritating groan and he said, "Open."

Crystal did as he instructed.

Then he pushed and prodded her neck and shoulders for lumps and bumps. "Does it hurt when I push here?" He touched her neck, back of her head and worked his way to the top of her head.

When he touched her temples, she jumped. "Ouch, that's bad!"

Mack jumped up and growled out, "Don't touch her anymore. Enough is enough!" He remained standing to protect her.

"I have to figure out what happened to her and the why. You need to sit back down sir, or you'll have to leave." The doctor stood firmly, his hands on his hips showing Mack he was serious.

Crystal smiled softly and touched Mack's arm. "It's okay. Let's figure this out, then we can talk, okay?"

Her soft angelic voice calmed him instantly. The doctor couldn't help hurting her during an exam. Mack sat down on the bed and held her left hand. "I'm sorry, doc. But, if you don't mind I'd like to sit here?"

The doctor nodded and smiled. "How long have you two been married?"

Mack coughed and cleared his throat. "Sorry, doc, we're not."

The doctor had pulled out a tablet. "Oh, sorry misunderstanding. You'd make a cute couple." He clicked a few times with a stylus on the pad then turned it towards her. "Crystal, this part of your brain is bleeding."

The word bleeding alerted Mack and he instantly reacted by moving around in his chair. He squeezed her hand, leaned down and brushed the hair away from her face, tucking the lose strands behind her ears as he'd witnessed her doing over the past years.

***

At the doctor's words, Crystal found her heart beating against her ribs. She felt frightened. Her body chilled, shivering and hot then sweaty at the same time. She was thankful when Mack reached out and gripped her hand. The friendship, love, strength and courage of this great man made it possible for her to refocus on the doctor. She finally knew she was in love with him and wanted to be with him forever. She'd known for a long time he loved her as much but only once did he ever bring up the subject and it was right after high school when her career had started to take off. She remembered clearly, when she told him they would have to wait and that was when she'd almost killed what they had. "Okay, what, why and how do we fix it?"

"I've went over all the scans, MRIs, and the other doctor's notes. You're a healthy young lady, but until we get you hydrated and some nutrition in you, I don't feel comfortable in operating. I'm not sure, but I have to ask, have you fallen or hit your head in the past few days or week?"

"Um… Well, a week or so ago, I tumbled down the stairs at home and hit this area." She touched the back of her head. "I bumped this side of my head on the last step as I landed."

The doctor touched her left temple and pain lanced through her head, ricocheting across her skull. She nodded. "Yep, there."

"Okay." He stood and smiled. "You, young lady, have what we call a TBI, Traumatic Brain Injury. If the swelling or bleeding worsens, we'll have to drill a hole and drain the fluid. We'll give you medication for you to sleep and heal. You're going to be with us for a few weeks, at the minimum."

Her face pinched up and she shook her head from side to side.

The doctor shook his head right back at her. "Well, I'm sorry if you don't like it but it's the safest and the effectiveness of the drugs and rest will help you heal faster. I've heard from others, it's something you don't do."

"And, who would that be?" She murmured, glaring at Mack. The pain again bounced around. She closed her eyes as the migraine hit hard and fast, almost tearing her apart. She realized she would miss out on Christmas if she didn't heal quickly. She needed to tell Mack what he meant to her, right? This holiday season could be the best yet, if she could just admit to him how she felt.

The doctor cleared his throat once and she refocused or tried to on his stone cold face. "Yes, doctor. Sorry, this headache is bad."

"I understand." The doctor nodded then continued, "First, try not to do any sudden movements with your head, neck and upper body…"

***

Crystal left the hospital two weeks later. The tour bus stopped and the air brakes hissed. Waiting for the all the other people to disembark from the bus was her choice. Her bedroom sat at the back of the bus and she'd stayed there the entire trip home.

They had a long bus ride home. No flying allowed due to cabin pressure and high altitude. It seemed to take forever until she saw her driveway up ahead.

One good thing happened already…she felt better. Surviving the daily migraines had pretty much ended any strength she had during and after she left the hospital. The headaches finally subsided with the increased amount of rest she'd been forced to do on the trip home. Thankfully, the motion sickness was non-existent with the vertigo medication from the doctor.

The smell of the country, horses grazing in the pastures on the left and the forest on her right welcomed her home. She sat on the edge of her bed and gave herself time to get her land legs back a little better. The dizziness from her injury had been brutal and falling would be extremely embarrassing.

Mack had acted so overly protective, he literally drove her crazy, but in a good way. At least, she knew he truly cared about her.

"I'll help you into the house if you'd like," Mack yelled from outside the bus.

I think about him and there he is again. Loving him for who he was meant everything. Finally admitting to herself, he held the key to her happiness. She could tolerate the way he took charge and the way he made sure she was someone who took charge and didn't let people bully her around.

She knew Mack would leave soon after he made sure she was safe. He spent the next two days with her, making sure everything was taken care of first. The staff assignments, background checks and all his anal OCD stuff would be completed before he left. How could she let him walk away? She loved him and wanted to share her life with him.

She didn't think she could live without him any longer and realized how badly she wanted him to make love to her. That's how far the relationship had gone within her heart and soul. Unfortunately, he had no idea about her feelings and she wasn't sure how to tell him.

Opening the door, she nearly collided with the man who constantly occupied her thoughts "Oh, hey…Okay, Let's do this." Stepping down out off the bus, she was definitely taken by surprise. The entire estate had been decorated with lights, Christmas paraphilia and large yard scenes made with life size decorations, characters and her favorite statues. Someone went to a lot of work to make her feel good when she arrived home. The holidays were the worse for her. No family and nearly no friends. Being alone had been her choice, and in the music industry, as you begin to write, it becomes an awful way of life but she liked it.

She'd secluded herself away these past few years partly because of her career, but mostly because of the mental illness, clinical depression. Without her music, who knows where she would've ended up.

"You?" She wobbled her way out to the front door. Her legs still having a little difficulty catching up with her brain. "How?"

"Don't have a friggin' clue what you're talking about." He held out his elbow. "Here, let's take a walk."

She reached out and gathered him closer to her by gripping ahold of his arm. Her rock and solid strength that kept her safe during the past years. "Can we walk down by the lake?" She pointed to the side of the house. She'd purchased it the first year after her music topped the charts winning her first Grammy award.

Looking for this specific property took some time but she wanted to consider all her wants and needs before settling on the right one. When the CEO of a large local company retired and chose to move to a warmer climate, her realtor placed a bid and she was able to purchase the entire estate for cash.

The lakeshore had iced over, but since it had been an unusually warm fall, the lake itself wasn't frozen solid yet. Sweatshirt, jeans, gloves and a hat kept her warm along with her boots. He held onto her hand to give support until they reached the shore.

What more could she want in a life partner? Mack was sexy, virile, strong and gorgeous, which was an added bonus. Slowly turning her head away from the beautiful vision of the half frozen lake, she gazed right at him. What more could she want to look at, than Mack.

He stood there staring across the grand lake. "So, I was thinking, Crystal. You know, we've been working together for a long time now and I'm kind of tired of the same old job and I want to move on."

She couldn't believe what he was saying to her. "Really? Why? Are you bored?"

"No, I wouldn't say that. But I would say it's time to move into a bigger and better position. This one is still at the bottom of the security part of your team."

"What do you mean by that?"

Mack's brow creased and he seemed to be concentrating on a

man down the shore, some ways from them. He seemed to be testing the thickness of the ice or something.

She couldn't believe what he was saying. He was bored? "Are you leaving me?" She wanted to know what his plans were. She had three months to find someone else she could trust to protect her. Plus, she felt a heaviness in her chest, she could never replace him in her life.

He turned his full attention on her. "I'm not quitting, I just don't want to work for you any longer. I want us to be a couple. I want to tour with you and take care of you as a man would a woman."

"You're saying you want to have a relationship with me?" She held her hand over her heart. Did she hear him right? Was he asking her to be her boyfriend or possibly even husband?

"I can't search the grounds, house and area anymore as security. I don't want to leave you. Yes, I'm asking you to give me some time and I will prove to you how much I care for you. Please, don't tell me to leave and never to come back again?"

"Why would I do that?" She tried her hardest to keep her face still and her eyes locked with his. She loved this man and she'd thought he said for them to be a couple. She felt confused. He'd never talk to her about them being together while he'd been head of her security.

"Hey, forget it for right now. Let me walk you to the house. I'm staying at least, for a couple of days." He spun around and his arm snaked around her middle.

"Okay," she readily agreed and wondered if he felt scared, she would turn him down. Again. There'd been a time in their past when she'd done just that and she deeply regretted it.

They walked up to the house. His team had made sure everything was clear. No one, including the press was around her house. She loved that about him. He was thorough and complete and did his job well. "How will I ever replace you?"

"Oh, honey, you won't have to. I'll be here every second of every day, keeping close watch over the security team I assign to you.

I would rather have you spend more time home and possibly have a family eventually?" They'd been making their way back to the house when he dropped that bomb. He stopped her, wrapped his arms around her body and held on tightly as if he never wanted to let go His body was literally shaking.

His almost hesitating and nervous approach made her feel sorry for putting him through whatever she did in the past. But there was no easy way with love when it came to the heart.

She didn't mind the affection, passion, lust or love from this amazingly great looking man who'd proven over and over again he could take care of her. Everything intensified his hold on her heart. "I want to go inside; could you build us a fire?"

"Yes, I can do that."

They walked inside the large but cozy mansion. Walking into the foyer, she noticed the entire place was decorated with pine branches, lights and flowing green garland. The large at least twenty-foot, Christmas tree fit perfectly inside her living area with the high open ceiling next to the loft where there was a sitting room.

She stepped up to the loft. Holding onto the railing all the way up.

Mack followed behind to her ensure she didn't fall.

These were the same steps she'd tumbled down. Reaching the top, she held onto the railing and looked over. The beautiful decorating brightened her house, the large wall of windows was black from the night and the moon, high in the sky, was almost full tonight. She also could see the entire reflection of what she looked like in it glass with Mack standing behind her. His body seemed to be rigid and stiff, in a military stance. How could she make him relax and turn him into her lover?

She loved this house and she finally realized the only thing missing was the special man who would share it with. Mack was her protector, partner and someone she could love for the rest of her life.

"Let's get you to your room. You need to rest." He didn't allow her to argue, but instead picked her up, carried her downstairs, then directly to her bedroom.

She giggled. "You're such a beast." The teasing tone of her voice brought a frown to his face.

He seemed to relax a little as he laughed out loud. "You're awful, Crystal, do you know that?"

"Yep, bed, please." He laid her gently on top of her comforter. She knew he didn't want to cause her any further injury to her head and cause her pain. When he tried to leave, she grabbed his hand and begged, "Stay?"

"Uh, no." He shook his head from side to side.

She smiled. "Yes, come on? You afraid?" Crystal knew very well she was playing the old card like they used to do in junior high school.

"Oh, hell with it." He pulled his boots off and spread his body out on the bed next to her. "Come here." His arm reeled her body up against his. With his large hand, he cupped her head, she let him hold her gently. "Go to sleep, my angel."

The nickname he'd teased her with was actually her last name. Multiple times during their junior and senior year in high school, he'd renamed her his angel. She loved it and wouldn't want him to change anything about himself. She regretted the time it took for both of them to realize how much they loved each other.

This time, she was just going to go for it, "Mack, I have something to confess to you."

"What would that be?" he whispered. His body tightly wedged up against hers.

Crystal snuggled up beside him and waited a few moments but before she was able to say the words, she heard his gentle snore in her ear and loved it. Maybe she could listen to this every night for the rest of her life.

***

Mack planned his proposal perfectly. Tomorrow…on Christmas morning. Life couldn't be turning out any better for him. He had faith it would be so much more. Especially, if she accepted.

Mack had wanted to tell her how much he loved her during high school. Now, it seemed he'd made the best decision. Her career had taken off and she'd made it. The only thing missing from both of their lives was each other, joined together in marriage.

He walked out of the house, towards the large barn. He wanted make sure his present for her was all set up and ready. As long as he'd known her, she'd wanted to do this. Well, she was going to get every wish she'd ever wanted from him. Those days of foster homes and nobody to love her was over. He had that covered in every department.

***

Crystal woke to the morning sun shining in through the open curtains of her bedroom. It felt nice being home and she stretched like a cat would in the sunshine. Her head still hurt and she was still weak, but overall she felt better.

Christmas morning. Normally, it was just another day but today something seemed different, even though she had no idea why. She'd bought her staff Christmas gifts. This year, she'd done all of her shopping on-line while in the hospital. She loved the on-line stores. Everything swift and simple and with a click of a button, it all would even be gift wrapped.

She followed the great scent of breakfast and found Mack in the kitchen dressed in jeans, t-shirt and an apron. Surprised, she giggled. "Hello there. You know, I never thought I'd see you in an apron."

He frowned. "Well, I didn't want to get my good clothes dirty. We have church remember?"

"I have something for you." She grinned.

"Well, I have something for you too, but you need to eat breakfast first." He dished up their plates and brought hers over to the table. "Sit."

"So demanding." She grinned. No pain, wonderful. Today would be a great day.

After they ate, she got up, walked into the living room, picked up the small wrapped package and slipped it into her pocket.

"Let's go." He'd already put his boots on and waited by the door. Every year, the tradition was church, then presents.

***

A few hours later…

The sermon had been beautiful, warm, wonderful, bright, and uplifting, Pastor Jameson did a great job.

On the way out, the Pastor stopped her. "Crystal Angel, we would love for you to maybe perform here even just once before you go back on your tour?"

"We'll see. Wonderful service, sir." She shook his hand.

He seemed polite but just a little too pushy. She'd sung in the church choir for as long as she remembered and he'd never acted like she'd been anything special, until she was to the world, apparently. It was kind of rude asking, begging and trying to get her to sing at church. She really didn't mind.

It did seem to bother Mack a little. He stood beside her and grunted, then grabbed her hand and guided her down the stairs and towards him pickup.

She hurried him along because she didn't want a scene as almost every year something or someone pissed off Mack whenever they pushed at her or wanted too much from her. He stopped beside a small group of women, smiled and said, "Mavis, Sylvia and Nancy, it's good to see you all."

The women smiled and nodded at him.

"Crystal, if you don't mind, I'd like to step over and talk to the Pastor. I have a few requests for him. Okay?"

His smile and warmth charmed her and made her feel loved and definitely not alone.

The women drew closer and were talking with her about her last tour.

Out of the corner of her eye, she spied Mack taking the pastor to the side. When the man smiled then nodded, she wondered what they would be talking about. After all, Mack had just looked angry with the pastor. They shook hands before Mack walked back over to her.

"Did you have nice visit with these beautiful young ladies?"

Mavis giggled, Sylvia and Nancy both put their wrinkled hands on Mack's arms. "We certainly did. Maybe you could join us for a Christmas dinner?"

"Sorry, but we already have a commitment waiting back at the house." He smiled and kissed their hands. Then he threaded their fingers together and tugged on her hand gently. "Are you ready?"

Crystal nodded, as she felt amazed. Mack's excuse to the churchgoers and ladies had dismissed them immediately. It was a nice reaction for once. She'd always tried to come up with excuses when they tried to keep her on the front walk too long. Somehow, he'd told the truth and they seemed to take his word.

***

When they arrived back at her estate, something definitely appeared odd. Nothing was making sense to her right now. She knew it seemed a little peculiar and her mind seemed to be spinning a little faster than normal but all in all everything seemed to be in order.

When the SUV didn't pull up the long drive to the house, but took the path to the barn she definitely knew something was going on and Mack was behind it. "What are you doing?"

"Shush, it's a surprise."

She smiled but kept her mouth closed.

The closer to the barn they drove, the more curious she got about something being inside it for her.

They pulled up to the barn.

"Well, come on." Mack grabbed her hand after opening the passenger side door.

She happily let him lift her up and gently set her down on the ground. When they entered, it felt like she'd been transferred into a fairytale.

All the Christmas characters of her favorite movies were there. Cat in the Hat, Nemo, Snow White and all the dwarfs, plus many more Disney characters and Snoopy statues. In the middle of all of it, a large carriage with two large white horses waited for them quietly. A man with a black top hat sat on the bench seat waiting for them to get inside.

Mack walked her to the carriage. "Before you get in, I have a question."

She nodded, her voice seemed to be stuck somewhere.

He pulled out a red rose from a vase. Attached to the stem was a ring, small, delicate but totally her. He knelt down and asked, "I felt like I didn't make it clear enough before, so here goes…Will you, please, agree to be my wife?"

Crystal felt her heart pounding almost loud enough to deafen her. Tears filled her eyes. "Of course, I'll marry you." She leaned down and kissed him.

They wrapped their arms around each other and shared a long passionate kiss. After she hugged him one more time, he helped her up in the carriage. "Merry Christmas. I love you so much," Mack said as he settled her in the seat.

Crystal couldn't believe how lucky she was. She pulled the box out of her purse and handed it to him. It was as if fate propelled them both, it seemed. "Merry Christmas to you as well."

Taking a deep breath, he opened it. Inside was a gold band with their names on it.

"Maybe you can wear this as your wedding ring?" she asked.

Mack nodded, and couldn't seem to speak as a single tear slipped from his eye.

Crystal wiped it away with her thumb. "I love you so much."

The End

ABOUT THE AUTHOR

Lanna Farrell has two beautiful daughters, a son-in-law, whom she adores and two gorgeous grandchildren. She enjoys time together with her family, curled up with a good book or saving any and every animal in her path. Her two dogs are her constant companions and she spends most of her time writing, reading or working as an author. As she recovers from her mental illnesses, PTSD being a large part of her life, writing helps her as she creates characters who can relate to what she suffers on a daily basis.

Born and raised in Minnesota, she will continue her life in the state with 10,000 lakes, along with the green grass, parks, and other exciting scenic attractions that bring people to the state. Winter wears on her soul but because her children have created their lives here she'll remain to stay close to them.

Finding herself retired from the trucking industry far too early because of a debilitating and crippling accident, she pushes on and continues to write. Her friends and family will contest to the fact she is never too far away from pens, paper or her computer.

Lanna is grateful to have joined the families of JK Publishing and especially excited about joining the family of Naughty Nights Press where she is gaining knowledge on how to create better stories with the help of their staff.

She can find so many things in this world that pique her interest and are inspirations to create entire stories.

To contact her, she can be reached at lannafarrell.com or join her on Twitter@lannafarrell67, or lanna.farrell.facebook.com.

If you're new to Lanna go to her website and sign up for the FREE books. This will give you a start to a library written specifically for her new readers.

She's taken the time to do book signings in North St. Paul, and in October 2016 she'll be at the Midwest Book Lover's Unite Convention in Bloomington, Minnesota. Come on down and see her. She'll be on a few panels and have her own table at the book signing. If you'd like to say Hi email her at lannafarrell@gmail.com.

BEST LAID PLANS
Diane Wiggert

Carl's Lake - Spring Lake, MN

"I really stepped in it this time, Fluffy." Evan Hovland absently stroked the broad head of his best friend with one hand while the other held his fishing rod. "It's okay though. I have a plan."

Fluffy, an English bulldog lifted her head, revealing a puddle of drool on the plywood floor of the ice fishing house. She raised her paw and scratched her ear causing the pink satin bow around her neck to sit askew.

"You have to leave it on," he said as he reached down to straighten the girly accessary. The glint of the icy stone on the ring he'd looped into the bow, cast rainbows around the small wooden structure. "Good girl."

Close to his home in Lakeville, Minnesota, this was perfect place to get away for some peace and quiet, with more fish than he could eat. "What better place to pop the question?" Evan looked around at the plywood walls, camp chairs, space heater, the holes in the floor for the lines and the cot on the end wall.

Not fancy but this was where they met and fell in love four years ago. Carl's lake, his favorite place to be in the winter. "Okay, it would be better if she were here, but she will be. Soon." Preferably, of her own choice but desperate men can't be choosy. "I will apologize, she'll call me an idiot and tell me what I did wrong, then she'll forgive me. If that doesn't work, I'll beg."

Life was good, great even—almost perfect. Or, it will be as soon as he figured out why Maya packed up her frog collection and left their townhouse three days ago. He knew she was serious this time when he found the bedroom dresser empty that normally held dozens of frogs in every shape and size. She'd been collecting them since her tenth birthday. The glass statue of a frog puckering up was the last gift she'd received from her father. He'd been killed later that year by a car while performing a routine traffic stop.

Christmas Eve dinner was only two days away. He thought announcing their long anticipated engagement would be the best present he could ever give to their parents with the exception of a grandchild someday.

"Yup, right on track. Engaged at thirty, married by thirty-one and kids by thirty-five. Well, the two legged kind that is." He gave Fluffy some full-length rubs to show her some love.

The sound of ice and snow crunching under tires alerted him to a truck stopping outside the fish-house. He grabbed Fluffy's jowly face with both hands exclaiming gleefully to the dog, "Who could that be?"

Fluffy panted her pink tongue rolling in and out, adding droplets of drool to the puddle already on the floor.

"Could it be the conservation officer?"

One loud happy bark rang out in the small space before she broke free from his grasp and darted as fast as her stout legs could carry her the four feet to the door.

The forceful knock made Evan's smile slip a fraction of an inch. What if it's not her? No, it had to be her. He'd called her partner and made sure she was working tonight. Wiping the moisture from his hands on his jeans, he took as much air into his lungs as possible before expelling it all in a long slow breath. Calmer, if only marginally, he opened the door. "Maya, hi." Like an ice statue, he stood frozen in the doorway with the northwestern wind sending a flurry of white stinging flakes into his face.

Great. What happened to the speech he and Fluffy had practiced over and over until it was tattooed on his frontal lobe? He couldn't even kick-start his brain at this moment with her standing less than five feet away.

A few strands of her raven hair defied the braid he knew she favored while working and slipped out from under her mad bomber hat. Her cocoa colored eyes bore into him as she absently reached down to stroke the dog with a gloved hand.

"Come in." He finally moved back, allowing her to enter.

She didn't move, but straightened and cocked her head to the side as if contemplating whether she should chance the step through the gates of hell or run for her life.

God, he hoped she would take the step.

***

Maya stood appraising Evan. She could see where this could lead, she'd come in and he'd apologize and she would forgive the sexy lug, and end up making ice melting sex on that rickety cot. Not this time. She would be strong.

"Come in, Maya. Please." He ran a hand through his golden waves.

Damn them puppy dog brown eyes. She didn't know who was better at the sad eyes, Evan or Fluffy. She stepped inside, waiting for it.

"Honey, I'm sorry." He took hold of her hand and pulled her a step closer to his heat. "I was an idiot."

She stayed quiet long enough to make him squirm. She would bet her lucky frog earrings he had no idea what he'd done. Again. And this was part of the problem.

Evan must have taken her silence as forgiveness because his features relaxed and the dimple in his right cheek appeared as his lips split into a killer smile.

God, she loved his smile. She knew she should say something, and was about to open her mouth to tell him what a complete jerk he'd been. As a grown woman of twenty-eight, she could make her own decisions, but his next move caught her off guard.

He dropped to one knee and pulled her hand free of her glove.

She froze.

"You remember that night, the blizzard?" He didn't wait for her reply. "You came to the door of this very fish-house to warn me about the storm. I lost my heart that night, I didn't know it for a few months but now I do. It was the first time I laid eyes on you and those warm brown eyes of yours melted my heart." Taking in a deep breath, he shuddered a little when he released it as a slow sexy smile light his face. "I love you, Maya Jo Henry, with all my heart." A wet nose nudged her hand and Evan laughed softly. "Fluffy loves you too. Marry me, Maya. Share my life and Fluffy's too." He slipped the bow from the dog's neck and held the ring up to her with love shining in his eyes.

Yes, it might just be the most beautiful proposal ever, almost perfect. Almost. She loved him but she wasn't sure if she could marry him. She looked him straight in the eye. "I love you, Evan. But…I don't know if I can marry you. Now or ever."

"What?" His smile dropped from his face and he stood. "I know what I did was stupid and inconsiderate, but I'm sorry, Honey, I swear."

She stepped back from him and crossed her arms in front of her. "Evan, do you know why I left?"

He too stepped back, pocketed the ring, then shoved both fists into his front pockets. "I said I was sorry."

"But do you know what for?"

His eyes darted around the small space before they settled on her face again. "I should have called. The guys wanted to have a couple drinks and I didn't know it would be so late." When she just stood there waiting he continued, "Okay, I knew, but it was only one beer. Two. Two beers."

"You think I left over a couple beers with your buddies? What kind of shallow witch do you take me for?"

He doesn't get it. I've made everything so easy for him. Always went along with his plans. What would he do if I resisted? Would he still love me?

***

Crap! Evan had no idea why she'd gotten mad. He didn't really think it was his monthly outing with the guys, which had set her off, but he really was clueless. Now he'd pissed her off and insulted her all in one stupid comment.

"You're right. You would never be that way and I didn't mean to imply you were." He wanted to pull her close, pull the hat off her head and work his fingers through her hair to loosen the braid. It always relaxed her, but she didn't look like he would get even a little finger on her dark trusses for a while. Evan scratched his head then looked up sheepishly. "So it probably wasn't the jade frog Fluffy broke last week?"

Her expression turned incredulous. She glanced down at the dog who stood no taller than her thigh. "Fluffy broke my figurine that sat on a shelf five feet in the air?"

"Okay, maybe I was the one to break it, but it was because I tripped on her bone. I've told her a thousand times not to leave it beside the bed."

"Ugh! Really. You're blaming the dog?"

"Hey, I fixed it. I bet you couldn't even see where I super glued it together. That stuff works like a charm."

Maya shook her head. "OMG, you are such a toad. I really do collect frogs," she muttered the last to herself.

He did hear her muttering. "I'll buy you another. I'm sorry." He chanced a step closer and touched her cheek. The soft stroking motion of his thumb had the fury in her eyes banking a little, so he gently drew her into his arms. "Maya, Honey, I may not know why you're mad at me but I know I really screwed up this time. Please tell me what I did. I promise not to do it again. I love you."

She let out a breath and as her shoulders dropped, so did her gaze.

Seeing his opening, he pulled her even closer and kissed her temple. He wiggled his nose as the fur of her hat tickled him but he didn't sneeze. Proceeding cautiously, like a man walking on thin ice, he placed another whisper of a kiss on her nose then captured her full lips, like he had wanted to from the moment he opened the door.

***

The barriers Maya erected lasted a full five seconds before his firm full lips had her own opening to him. The slide of his tongue, the way he nibbled on her lower lip, she knew it would be only a matter of minutes before she would be down to her bra and panties. He had a command over her body and could relax or excite her with a touch of his fingertips. He entranced her and she loved it.

She felt her hat fall from her head and a moment later, heard the zipper of her coat. Her body went compliant, but her mind kept working hard to remember why she left this man. He sure seemed like a man with a plan though, and when his cold fingers brushed her side as he worked her shirt free from her pants, she froze. Her brain engaged and she raised her hands to stop him. "No," she spoke softly but that was all it took for him to stop.

Evan spun away from her and fisted both his hands into his hair. His frustrated grumble filled the fish-house. '

She picked up her hat and rezipped her coat.

"Why?" He spun back around, his mood turned to frigid in a blink of an eye. "We've been together for three years. I know you. When I piss you off, we yell and you go to your sister's house. I know the only reason you stay the night is because you have a glass of wine while you vent. Hell, we've never had a serious fight, so why now? Christmas week you pack up and run for the hills?"

"You're right. We've never had a major fight, and that's my fault." She was tired of always giving in. Yes, he would apologize if she became angry but did she ever get her way when it really mattered? Maya pulled on her gloves. "Evan, you really have no idea why, do you?"

He shook his head.

"Well, let's just say it's my turn to make the decisions and I'm starting with Christmas dinner with my family." She turned, gave Fluffy a brisk rub then walked out the door.

Back in her truck, crossing the lake she felt the sting of fresh tears. She knew it was stupid and Christmas wasn't the whole reason, but she couldn't bring herself to tell him the real reason. She wasn't sure if he loved her for the woman she was or for the fact that she fit into his ten-year plan. He'd been honest about his plans and had never made her feel like just a body filling a spot, but the woman he loved. Lately though, her emotions were driving the bus and she couldn't say if the sweet, sexy man she loved with all her heart…loved her back with his.

"It has to be the holidays." She wiped her tears on her sleeve. But whatever it was, she couldn't be with him until she knew for sure this was the real deal for him too, with or without his almighty plan.

Picking her phone up from the seat, she called her mother. When she heard her mom's voice on the machine, her tears started to flow. "Mom, I'm coming home for Christmas."

***

"Crap, crap, crap! Now what do I do?"

Fluffy tilted her head and let out a snort.

"I know." Evan nodded. "She's not herself lately and she won't tell me what's going on." He dropped down into the chair knocking his fishing rod to the ground. He dropped his head into his hands. "I'm screwed, and my Christmas surprise is ruined." He'd tried giving her space and it hadn't worked. Paws landed on his knees and a wet tongue slurped across his face. He caressed the dog's wide head as he worked on a plan to win her back.

"Christmas!" He laid a big smacking kiss on the canine's nose. "I have to call the family. First, I need to call Joan." Maya's mom and sister were coming to Christmas at his parents. It was going to be a surprise for Maya and the perfect time to tell the whole family about the engagement. Two days. He had to work fast.

In the next hour, Evan closed up the fish-house, called Maya's mom and sister and was on his way to his parent's house in Prior Lake.

He walked in the door without knocking and hollered from the entry, "Mom, Dad, anybody home?"

Fluffy strolled right in and found her favorite spot on the dog bed grandma left for her in front of the stacked stone fireplace.

"In the kitchen." Maureen, his mom, was making a batch of rosettes and the place smelled like Christmas's past.

He carefully came up behind her at the stove, not wanting to cause an accident with the hot oil, and kissed her cheek.

She turned and with one look at his face, turned off the burner and stepped away from the stove. "What is it?"

He could never hide anything from her.

"Come, sit." She guided him to the kitchen chair and went back to retrieve a couple bottles of water from the fridge then sat in the seat across for him. She said nothing. The very same tactic she'd always used to get him to confess to everything from skipping school to how the dent really got onto the back bumper on Dad's car.

He knew it would spoil his surprise but at this point, there wouldn't be one anyway. "I proposed to Maya."

"Oh, Honey. I'd say that's wonderful but the look on your face tells me it didn't go well. What happened?" She stroked his arm and waited.

"She left three days ago. She didn't take everything but... she took her frogs."

"Oh, no."

Evan filled her in on the events of the last week and what happened at the lake. "Is there a chance we can move Christmas dinner up north to Joan's house?" It was a lot to ask to move the whole family two days before the holiday. Ten people in all if you counted his brother Jamie's family.

"I'll handle it, don't worry. You have enough to do to convince Maya to marry you." She stood, came around the table and stopped in front of him. "You know I love Maya, but I have to ask." She hesitated, picked up his hand then looking him in the eye with the *don't-you-dare-lie* look. "I know you are very driven and if you have a goal, you don't stop until you achieve it. I'm proud of the way you stepped up and are running Hovland Electric with your father. You need to ask yourself one thing, do you just want to be married or do you want to be married to Maya?" She patted his hand as she stepped back, gave him the old wizard look and left the kitchen.

Of course, he wanted to be married to Maya, why would she even ask that? He loved her and couldn't imagine his life without her. He'd been lucky she'd came into his life that stormy night and it'd been purely coincidence the timing worked with his plan.

Hearing Fluffy's snore from the living room made him feel sad. He should be home with Maya, listening to the nasal sounds of his dog. Why would Maya leave? He glanced over his shoulder to see his mother in the next room with the phone to her ear. Such a wise woman and it had taken him a quarter of a century to realize that fact.

"Crap on a cracker! Could Maya wonder if I wanted her for her? Well, that's just freakin' great. How do I get her to understand it's only her?"

"Have you told her? And not with words," his mom yelled from the living room.

"That makes no sense."

"Show her," this time she spoke softly. She crossed the room and hugged him from behind.

"How?" He reached up and returned the embrace.

"You'll figure it out. You're a smart boy."

Evan wasn't sure how, but damn it, he would and in the next two days.

***

Maya finished her shift the next day and headed home for the holidays. When her mom called back, she seemed surprised and happy to hear of her visit, but a little concerned.

Joan met her at the door with a huge hug and her sister, Jolie, carried her bag in. "Let's get you out of all that winter gear and into some comfy pajama pants." Joan led the way to her old room overlooking the creek, which ran through the back of their property.

She missed the Pequot Lakes area but loved her life in the cities. With parks and lakes covering more than thirteen million acres of the state, her job options were unlimited. The fact that Evan lived there was a main reason she hadn't moved home. She loved him. He had faults but even his cluelessness and his take charge demeanor didn't bother her most of the time. It'd only been recently she'd started questioning his love. The man with a plan. They joked about it, but the more she thought about it, the more she wondered if he would still love her if she veered from his long-term plans.

Once she changed clothes, she made her way to the kitchen.

Her mother and sister were already seated at the table with three mugs of steaming coffee in front of them and a plate of cut-out cookies.

Maya sat and claimed one of the mugs. "Mmm, thanks. You always know how to cheer me up," she added as she reached for a sugary snowman.

"Okay, now you have sugar and caffeine. Now spill." Jolie had no patience.

Maya wasn't sure how to explain, so she started at the beginning, "I needed a little space to figure some things out so I packed my frogs, a small bag and moved into a coworker's house. She'd asked me to check on it while her family is away." She tried to keep it short and to the point but when she told them about the proposal in the fish-house, she couldn't stop the flood of tears. Over the last week, she had cried more than she had in ten years of chick flicks, and she loved a good sappy movie cry.

Her mom and sister glanced at each other but neither said a word.

"What aren't you telling me?" Maya pulled the collar of her t-shirt up and wiped her face.

"Aren't you being a little hard on Evan? I mean, have you told him how you feel?" her mother asked before passing the plate of cookies to her.

"This is nothing new. He has his plans and if he wants to do something he does it, not asking what I want." She took a snowflake shaped cookie this time and before her mom pulled the plate away, she grabbed a Santa one too. She shoved the first one into her mouth then mumbled around the sugary treat, "Last March, the Cancun trip. That was his idea, deep-sea fishing. I wanted to go on a cruise."

"Did you tell him that?" Joan asked as she swept up crumbs with her hand.

"Yes."

Jolie didn't even try to cover her scoff. "No, you didn't." Maya opened her mouth to interject but her sister continued, "I was at dinner with you guys the night he brought it up. He said 'let's do a Mexican vacation, some beach time, some drinks and dancing and a little deep sea fishing' and then you suggested a cruise. He said something about finding one with a deep sea fishing shore excursion and you went all marshmallow and said, 'No Babe, Mexico sounds fun. We can do a cruise next year.' I thought you had a great time on that trip?"

"We did." She had no idea why it bothered her now. "Not the best example." She pursed her lips and tapped them with her finger. "Okay, he bought a new truck without consulting me first."

"You mean the F-150?"

She nodded at her mother's question.

"The one he bought two years ago when you weren't living together yet?"

Maya deflated, crossed her arms on the table and dropped her head down. "I'm a bitch. What's wrong with me?"

She felt the soft caress of her mother's touch. "Baby Girl, it's an emotional time for you. My moods were up and down, too, when I was expecting you. Evan loves you and I think you need to talk to him."

"What? No, Mom, I'm not pregnant." Her head flew up in time to see the sweet smile on her mother's face.

"My mistake." Joan picked up the mugs and carried them to the sink.

"I'm tired, I think I'll turn in. Thanks for the snack," she said as she headed for her room.

Pregnant? It can't be. She just had her period the week before Thanksgiving. Coming to a dead stop in the middle of the hall, she started counting. "Uh, Fudge!" she muttered. It could be. Tomorrow morning she would run out to the store before they closed for the holidays and pick up a test. Wouldn't that throw Evan's ten-year plan into a tailspin?

She closed the door to her room, curled up on the bed and started to rock. Was her mother right? Had she'd been worrying for nothing and Evan loved her, and not his life plan? If so, everything would work out fine. If not? She started to cry. *Again.*

***

The next morning, Evan started his long drive up north with positive thoughts and enthusiasm. By the time he hit Brainerd, he was a wreck. His family traveled together in two vehicles, his parents rode with him and Fluffy while his brother and his family followed. Three hours of his father talking golf, his mother knitting in the backseat of his truck and Fluffy snoring was more than enough family time for him. Plus, he still had to make it through dinner and gifts with his brother's kids. Three and five-year-old boys. He loved them but they had one volume—loud.

Evan still wasn't sure what he was going to say to Maya to convince her he truly loved her and he wanted to spend his life with her. He'd practiced for weeks on the first proposal and obviously, it hadn't worked out the way he'd hoped. Maybe this time, he should just try to convince her to move back in, and then he could work on another proposal.

As they turned off the highway and neared the house, Evan hoped Joan and Jolie were able to keep their arrival a secret.

Fluffy sat up, gave a low whine and a happy bark as she recognized Grandma Joan's house. The truck coasted to a stop in front of the cedar-tone rambler.

Joan had decorated the windows and door with evergreen boughs and white lights, which framed the tree in the living room to create the picture perfect holiday look. After helping his mother out of the truck, he made two trips to the door to carry all the packages inside. Evan stood on the threshold, took a cleansing breath then stepped through.

Joan stepped up and pulled him into a warm welcoming hug then dropped to give Fluffy loving attention.

Evan's gaze scanned the room looking for Maya.

"She's in the basement," Joan interjected. "I sent her downstairs to wrap a last minute gift when I saw you pull up."

"Might as well let you get in the door before the fireworks start," Jolie stated as she came in for a hug. "Talk to her," she whispered in his ear.

"That's the plan." He nodded.

Jolie shook her head. "No plan, just talk." She gave him one more squeeze before carrying the gifts to the living room to place under the tree.

Right, no plan. Good thing, too, because all coherent thoughts left his brain when Maya walked into the room.

Her hair hung loose around her shoulders and she wore a red sweater that brought out the rosy glow in her cheeks. But those beautiful chocolate eyes looked so sad.

Evan wanted to scoop her up and kiss her under the mistletoe, or anywhere for that matter. He watched the shutters come down and the sadness disappear at the sight of him. For a fleeting moment, he thought he saw joy, but it disappeared too fast for him to tell. He half expected her to leave the room, but she squared her shoulders and walked straight toward him.

***

"I should have known it was you when Mom said we were having company," Maya said as she crossed the room. She folded her arms under her breasts, and didn't miss the quick trip his eyes took down her body.

"You wanted to have Christmas with your family. You left before I had a chance to tell you I'd invited them to my parents this year. Surprise!" He stepped closer and dropped his voice a few decibels. "I'd also hoped we could gift our parents with the announcement of our engagement." He gave a single laugh. "Ha. I guess that isn't going to happen."

When she'd asked why the table was set with so many plates, her mother had told her she'd been planning to go to a friend's for the holiday but invited them here when Maya called and said she was coming home. They were going to surprise her? The lump that settled in her throat stopped any words from coming out. This wasn't the place for a private conversation. She tipped her head toward the hall and started for her room.

Both he and Fluffy followed.

Once in the bedroom, she closed the door partway.

Evan cleared his throat and reached for her hand.

She let him take it.

"Maya, I don't need to be married. I mean, would I like us to get married… Hell yes! That way every guy out there knows what a lucky SOB I am to have you." He moved in and she could feel his warmth radiating through her sweater. "It's you. You, I want by my side always. You I love." He cradled her face with his hands never breaking eye contact. "I'll do whatever you want."

Inside, her heart was jumping for joy, but her brain still had concerns about his plans. "What about your ten-year plan?"

"None of it matters without you."

"So, if we never marry and we live in sin, you're okay with that?"

"Yes, I'll live in sin with you any day," he answered with a wolfish grin.

She fought hard not to smile. Marriage wasn't the only thing that could throw off his plans. "And if I can't have children or decide I don't want them." This last part would be a stretch, he knew she loved kids and wanted a house full.

"If we can't, we'll adopt, and if you don't want any, we can have the four-legged kind." He stroked a knuckle down her cheek.

Maya stared at Fluffy on the bed, not meeting his eyes. "What if I were pregnant right now?" When he didn't respond, she chanced a look at his face.

His warm eyes melted as they gazed into hers looking for the truth. "Really?"

With the barest of movement, she nodded.

Tears misted his dark eyes and his arms encircled her in the most gentle and loving embrace. "A baby?"

Her nod was more pronounced this time. She opened her mouth to say yes but he took her very breath as he kissed her, long and firm, all the love and surprise he felt poured from him to her. His hands slid to her hips and he raised her up, so she could wrap her long legs around his waist. They stayed in that very spot kissing for so long, they lost track of time.

Jolie stuck her head in the room, then closed the door. She yelled back to the others in the living room, "Oh yeah, I'd say they made up."

Maya pulled back, a radiant glow lit her entire being. "Is that marriage proposal still on the table?"

"Hell, yes!" He set her down, whistled for Fluffy and then knelt to retrieve the diamond ring looped in her collar.

"I hadn't even noticed that."

Laughter sparkled in his eyes as he took her hand. "Maya Jo Henry, will you do me the honor of becoming my wife? Sharing all your joys and sorrows with me and making me the happiest man alive?"

She saw more than humor, his eyes held all the love she could ever hope for. Tears flooded down her cheeks, as she stood immobile.

"Will you marry me?"

She let out a sobbing breath as her head bobbed up and down. Then the words finally came, "Yes! I didn't think it could be better than your last proposal but it was."

"This one was way better. You said yes." He pulled her onto his knee and kissed her.

When she pulled back, he glanced at the snoring dog on the bed a few feet away. "Well, either I kick Fluffy off the bed and we celebrate the way I want to or we can go surprise the parents with the good news. Which do you choose?"

Maya stared at the bed. She would pick the first one in a heartbeat if both their families weren't a frog's leap away from them, to say nothing of the way sound traveled in the small house. "I suppose we should go be social."

Evan kissed her nose then helped her stand as he rose from the floor. He pulled her into his arms for a quick kiss then reaching into his pocket, he pulled out a small foil wrapped box.

"What's this?" Her eyes were tearing up as he held it out to her.

"Your Christmas present. I planned to propose at the fish-house, not on Christmas. Open it." He prodded as she stared at the box in her hand with tears streaming down her cheeks. He wiped her face with his sleeve and placed a gentle kiss on her forehead.

She carefully removed the tape and unfolded the paper, then cracked open the lid, peering inside as the next flood of tears started. "It's perfect. It's you." She laughed through her tears as she held up the crystal pendent. A puckering frog with a gold crown. "My prince."

Handing it to him, she turned around, so he could clasp the necklace for her. Then she turned back and beamed. "What do you think?"

Evan's eyes roamed her body from the top of her head to her slipper covered toes, stopping to linger at her stomach then his intense gaze swung back up to rest on her eyes. "You're beautiful."

His voice sounded a little husky to her. Raw. She might even say froggy.

He cleared his throat, took her hand and gave her a quick hard kiss. "Come on, I smell the delicious ham your Mom made and you need to eat." Evan led her from the room.

Maya smiled to herself as they left the room with Fluffy on their heels. *That's my prince.*

ABOUT THE AUTHOR

Diane Wiggert writes contemporary romances with heart, humor and hometown heroes. When she's not writing or reading, she's elbow deep in a home improvement project. She enjoys seeing new places whether by car, plane or through a book, but her favorite place is the small Minnesota town where she lives with her husband, son, and crazy canine.

Best Laid Plans is her fourth short story. Her other works include *Spring Thaw* in Romancing the Lakes of Minnesota-Spring anthology, *Magic at Moose Lake* in Romancing the Lakes of Minnesota-Autumn anthology, and *Love's No Joke* in the Romancing the Lakes of Minnesota-Winter anthology.

You can follow Diane on Facebook, Twitter or Google+.

CHRISTMAS JOY
Rhonna Krueger

Lake Minnetonka - Wayzata, MN

Dedication

I dedicate this book to all my family and friends. Happy Holidays to all of you and I hope you have a wonderful December and time with your family and especially time spent going to church and praising our Jesus Christ. Many people forget this holiday is in celebration of his birth.

The Lord replied.
"My presence will go with you,
and I will give you rest."
Exodus 33:14

The aroma of the blended brands of coffee was like heaven to her nose. Joy Abraham sat in her favorite chair at the coffee house she'd spent hours in when escaping from reality and writing. Her laptop opened in front of her with a story about a young woman who finds her happily ever after and all that crap. Why she was still writing romance was beyond her. She hadn't had a great track record when it came to relationships in a long time, the last time was probably high school and it had been one-sided…hers.

Reeling from her thoughts, she knew part of it was the mental illness she suffered from. Maybe a trip to the doctor was needed. It had been a while since she'd been in for a medication recheck. Always around the holidays, she'd end up in a funk. Especially, since she lost her mom and now, the health issues with her dad.

Again, she lost her thoughts in the romance story open in front of her. Her mind filled with everything going on in her life right now. She looked around the coffee shop surrounded by cheery holiday decorations, which were depressing to her.

The back of her eyes burned from unshed tears. If she hadn't grown up so quickly and sternly she would probably be sitting in a chair right now sobbing like a small child.

Realistically, she knew that wasn't going to happen because she had just too much to do. The book wasn't due until the twenty-ninth of December. It wasn't too far off but enough time to finish the eighty-thousand-word story. The first three thousand sat in front of her but she had writers block a mile thick.

The sudden memory of what actually brought her here from New York invaded her mind. She'd arrived back here, to Lake Minnetonka in the town of Wayzata yesterday. Her father had taken a turn for the worse and it was time to put him in a home worthy of taking care of him. In his younger days, he'd been a brilliant heart surgeon, now he had to wear diapers and couldn't remember to eat. Someone needed to remind him to eat food, take his medication, and even to go to bed where he would try and sleep. A strict routine helped keep the disease from progressing even further.

The new home she'd chosen was beautiful, elegant, and classy enough where he would be able to live out the rest of his life comfortably.

Today was the day she had to put her mentor, father and greatest man she'd ever known into a care facility to be monitored and cared for because no way was she experienced enough with Alzheimer's to do it herself.

She gave up and closed her laptop. Stuffing it into her large bag, she threw it over her shoulder and walked to the front counter.

Katie handed her the iced latte she'd bought earlier. The girls here knew her so well, from coming and going the past five years. "Thanks, Katie girl."

The young girl nodded.

Joy threw a twenty-dollar bill into the tip jar.

Katie's eyes widened and she yelled out, "Merry Christmas, Joy. Hope to see you tomorrow."

She waved over her head. "We'll see, busy days ahead of me."

Nobody knew what she faced and Joy didn't share. Too much pain and heartache, she wouldn't want to ruin everyone's holiday cheer.

Driving back to the house where she'd grown up, she spotted the for sale sign larger than life already in the front lawn. She'd planned on asking Pete, the driver to leave through the backside of the mansion, which faced the lake. They needed to leave shortly and take her father to his new home. It was tearing her heart in two.

Pete Anderson, the driver was a great friend and if she were honest with herself, she would admit she'd had a crush on him since as far back as she could remember. Back in high school, he'd been tall and gangly, now his body had filled out nicely and he was still tall but bulked out, no fat and definitely more muscles than most normal men she dated. His high and tight hair was shaved, all but the top with maybe half of inch of hair. She loved his tanned skin and barely but faded beard with a thick goatee and tightened mustache that made him look so handsome. She couldn't believe the change in him. It actually made her want him even more now than before.

She was sad they actually went their separate ways right after graduating. Her a scholar and him, a jock who played every sport he could. They grew up together right here in this house. His family worked for hers.

Even though most of his family had to retire because of their age, Pete kept his job, taking care of the outside maintenance and being the family driver for everyone in the house. Her father hadn't driven himself in years. Being a heart surgeon, he'd never had time to drive to and from the hospital, but instead he'd done his charting in the car. When they went somewhere, it'd been easier to have a driver than worry about trying to find the places they'd constantly been invited to for all the parties and ceremonies.

She knew Pete and his family still lived on the property right in their own little house and his mom and dad worked still, doing a little here and there. But at their age, nothing was expected. As her dad had always said, "Once a faithful employee, they became part of the family." She had no arguments there.

This had been a tradition of how her parents did business. Everyone stayed a part of their family. Such a sad situation, now she had to let everyone go, especially after the sale of the house. She wanted to break down and bawl her eyes out. But she didn't have the time or energy to lose it completely.

Walking inside, her heels clicked on the tiled floors as she made her way to the sound of voices coming from the kitchen. Her father was sitting at the kitchen table arguing with the nurse they'd hired.

"Come on, Dr. Abraham, please take the medication, it will make you feel better." The nurse set the small cup on the counter and walked away

Joy shook her head. Then made her way over and sat down at the table. "Hey, you."

His eyes were bright with tears as they widened. "You've come home?"

"Yes, I'm home." Joy knew he spoke from the past. He didn't recognize her at all.

When he patted her outstretched hand, he whispered, "Lexy, I missed you so much."

"I know you do. Can you take the medication the doctor prescribed, please?" Joy hated letting her father think she was his wife. She'd lost her mother a few years ago to breast cancer.

"Of course."

Joy reached behind her for the medicine cup. Poured them in her palm and handed them to him. "Here you go."

"Thanks, dear." He gulped them down with his orange juice. "Eggs again?" he quietly asked.

"Those are your favorite." Joy kissed his weathered cheek.

"I know. Sometimes, I wish the cook would switch it up a bit. Maybe oatmeal for tomorrow?"

Joy nodded and smiled. She stood up and smoothed the little bit of his hair back on his balding head.

Sadness descended heavily on her over losing the greatest mind of all time. Her father, a retired heart surgeon, actually one of the top in the United States had to retire early because Alzheimer Syndrome had slowly taken his mind away. He'd retired from his field, only five years ago at the age of sixty-two. I'd been so sad to watch his mind shrivel and his body grow old. The disease was killing him slowly. Joy hoped the care facility would be able to help him live a little longer with a more fulfilled life. They knew exactly what to do to slow the process down.

After putting his dishes away in the dishwasher, she said, "Come on papa. Let's go upstairs and get you dressed. We have an adventure today that I know you'll love."

He pushed his way up from the chair using the table. "I love our outings; you know me so well, Lexy."

He'd began calling her Alexys or Lexy her mother's nickname, especially when his mind was away but if it returned, as it often did still, he would know she was Joy and he would again be saddened by the loss of his wife, Lexy.

***

Hours Later…

Joy, Pete, and her father gathered out front of the grand, enormous, beautiful home. On the outside, it appeared to be a mansion. On the inside it was a hospital and would cost Joy over eight thousand dollars a month to have him live here. They had doctors, nurses, physical therapists, etc. knowing exactly what and how to treat a patient with Alzheimer's.

"What is this place, Joy?" For the first time in hours, her father recognized her.

"Think of it as a great adventure, Daddy. Momma, me and you had checked this out for you, remember?" She prayed he would listen and not give them a fight. Pete could force her father but that wasn't what she wanted and neither did anyone else. The nurses inside said they could give him medication to calm him down, but she chose to try and reason with him.

Pete stepped forward. "Sir, I'd like to take a look, if I may. Will you join me?"

"Oh sure, Pete. It's great to see you again. It's been a while now hasn't it?"

Pete smiled, winked then nodded. "Yeah, it's been a bit, hasn't it?"

"You've grown into a handsome young fellow. Have you asked my daughter here, Joy out on a date yet?"

Pete shook his head.

Her father smiled, "Well, what's taking you so long. You know you've had a crush on her." Then he turned to her. "Joy, you've been in love with this boy for years. I remember—"

"Dad, come on, you're embarrassing both Pete and I. Let's go on inside." Joy's face had to be hundred different shades of red. Yes, she'd had a crush on Pete for as long as she remembered but always was way too shy to approach him. He was one of those popular kids in high school, but she'd been a nerd who, studied and read, all the time, alone.

Inside Joy crumbled. Her sadness doubled. Saying goodbye to Pete would be the worst of it all. Not only did she have to leave her father in this home, she also needed to get their family home sold. She could handle losing the house but to say goodbye to the only family, besides her parents, she'd ever had was another thing entirely.

On her author salary of fifty thousand a year, she couldn't even afford the taxes on the house, which were over fifteen grand a year. The upkeep and the employees' salaries were a whole other expense and there was no way she could afford it. It all needed to go.

Her bestseller author status made enough money to be comfortable but not enough to afford paying the rate the house required. "Pete?" she asked holding out her hand.

He reached out and took her hand.

It seemed nice to feel his warmth, causing her to relax and feel something she hadn't in a long time, love, understanding, and a friendship.

She felt saddened to leave her father here, but it was for the best. To try and keep him at their home had been too much. Not only expensive but the hired nursing and doctor staff, plus the extra care team needed to be there twenty-four-seven. All of it wasn't going to work. Besides, he needed the extra help because his type sometimes, got a little angry and violent.

"Come on. Let's go get settled in." Pete walked side by side with her to the administration office.

"Oh, Joy, how are you." Melissa Davis stepped out of her office.

"Is this your husband?"

Joy shook her head, her face hot and flushed.

"I'm a good friend to both Joy and her father, the name's Pete Henderson." He shook Melissa's hand.

"Well, come on in." Melissa led the way. Her father followed and stepped inside the office, timidly at first, then Melissa turned and said, "It's great to see you again, Dr. Abraham."

"Oh yeah, it's been a while." He looked at his watch with a twist of his wrist. "About, I'd say maybe five years or more," he mumbled.

"I remember when you and your wife came by and took a look at it for her to stay with us? Or was it something else?"

Joy didn't know that her folks had visited here.

"Oh, the misses expected someday soon that I'd need to stay here in a home like this. Actually, this was my favorite." He turned to Joy. "I suppose the time has come, hasn't it?" He seemed to be suddenly lucid. "Things are jumbled up here a little too much." He pointed to his head. "I tend to forget my wife has died and my brain just isn't as it should be. Alzheimer's is a tricky illness. You know I feel like there are good days, then I have days I'm not sure I remember even getting up in the morning or going to bed. It's kind of weird and a little scary." He leaned over and kissed Joy on the cheek. "You're a good daughter. This must be hard on you? But you have Pete here and he'll make sure to help you with everything that needs to be done."

Joy felt truly shocked at how clear her father's mind was at the moment. "Oh Daddy, I hate leaving you here."

Pete still had ahold of her hand, he squeezed it tightly, just enough to have her look up at him. He shook his head and with sad eyes nodded to her father.

She swallowed heavily. "Okay, Dad. You're happy with the choice you've made in staying here?"

"I am. Look, I know you have so much to do. I'm sure you have some history book or something like that you need to get done. Let this old man go to his little apartment upstairs and settle in. I'll give you a call tomorrow." Her father stood up and walked her to the door of the administrator's office.

"I love you, Daddy." She hugged him tightly.

He pulled away but still held onto her arms. "Joy, you've been wonderful through all of this. I hope this Christmas; you finally find what will make…" He pointed to her heart. "…You happy." He hugged her and whispered near her ear, "Find that man who you can say you've been married to for thirty years like I was able to do before your mom's passing. We were married young but we had a lot of good years together. Don't worry about me, I'll be fine right here. But when it's time." He winked at Pete. "I'd be honored to walk you down the aisle."

Joy kissed him one more time on the cheek and gave him a hug. Her eyes burned and she wanted to cry.

Then her father, always in control when his mind was doing okay, led the way out of the office and turned to Melissa. "Come on young lady, will you show me to my new home? The suitcases, I'm sure are already up there. All I have to do is put stuff away. Love you, Joy. See you soon." He walked away and didn't even look back. He was a stoic individual and wanted her to stand on her own two feet. Confident she'd be okay.

She knew the same was true about him. She felt relieved he wasn't in one of his episodes and confused, then it would have been hell to leave him.

Pete walked her to the car.

She looked back at the doors then at him. "Do you mind if I ride up front with you? I just can't sit back there by myself."

"Of course. Joy, I'm glad you're home. New York is too far away and I missed you." He politely opened the front passenger door for her to get in.

Her and Pete had been friends for as long as she could remember. He'd been quarterback in high school and all jock where she'd been the one to go to school, get really good grades, study and take all the hard core classes. She felt like they expected her to take after her dad but it was completely opposite. Her mom and dad coaxed her to take what she loved to do not what they did. She'd started out writing for a magazine in New York and made her way up to the New York Times as an editor. Her salary there had financed her author dream of writing romance.

***

Pete walked her inside the house.

"I just don't even know where to begin to start packing this monster," Joy said.

He stepped forward and wrapped his arms around her. "Joy, why don't you just take your time. You don't need to sell it, immediately. I think there's something I should show you."

"Okay." She nodded and followed him to her father's office.

On top of the desk, an oversized calendar lay spread out but that wasn't what held her attention. The letter with her single name, *Joy*, in her father's handwriting. Pete picked it up and handed it to her.

"What is this?" she asked.

"Your father had a really good week and this was something he asked my father to come in and help him with. They had a team of lawyers and everything. It's what your parents had planned for you all along. My father explained a little to me, but not much. If you want to share it with me, that's your choice. Otherwise, I'll leave you alone. Do you want something to drink?"

"A glass of ginger ale please, then will you come back in here and sit with me while I read this?"

"Sure."

After Pete brought back two tall glasses full of carbonated drinks, he walked up to the desk and sat down in one of the plush leather chairs in front of her.

Already seated in her father's big chair, she opened the envelope and started to read it aloud.

Joy, if you're reading this letter, your mother has passed and I've been put in a very expensive home you and your mom had chosen for me. The room and board has been paid for until my death. There is no reason for you to fret over losing the house or having to sell it. If you choose to stay, I've arranged a trust fund for all the employees' salaries for the next fifty or more years.

Your mother and I had always planned to take care of you, our dear sweet child, Joy. You were the only child your mother could conceive and you were our little princess. Take the money which is in all these accounts and live life to the fullest.

Find yourself a young man.

She stopped reading it out loud, too embarrassed, she continued on her own.

Pete, for example has had a massive crush on you since you turned sixteen or seventeen I can't remember exactly. But I do know both your mother and me concurred he's a perfect match for you and will help you manage this house and all the accounts. He won't steal from you or blow smoke up your behind. Your mom also confessed you told her how big of a crush on Pete you had. Go for it toots. It's a happy life to love someone to the fullest.

She looked up at Pete, smiled, and finished the letter out loud.

Take this time to take care of things here in the house. Enjoy your life to the fullest and make sure you always celebrate Christmas, no matter what. Decorate, invite friends, and do all the festivities as I've done for years in the past. Celebrate the life your mother and I gave you. We hope you get married someday and have the house full of children.

Even though I suffer from Alzheimer's, I'm still aware of you being my daughter and I've always wanted to make sure you had the life you were used to. The only condition I have is that you marry a man and enjoy life, have a family and take care of the house as your mother and I have always done.

Forever in peace and love. God Bless you, Joy.

The document was signed, notarized and legally submitted through the court system. Her father had account statements worth billions. How and what he'd done to have this kind of money in the bank she had no idea.

Her frown must have triggered Pete to speak, "I hope you read the letter and understand what your mom and dad wanted."

She nodded. "Pete, I'm in shock here. What in the world? How?"

"Your father was a great man. He developed a way to keep someone alive with a device that is hooked up to the heart and kept the faulty organ pumping until a transplant is available. The stock alone had always taken care of your family. He trusted my parents to help him manage the accounts and money. He chose to continue working as a doctor because he loved it. If the Alzheimer's hadn't affected him so quickly, I'm sure he'd still be working." Pete laughed.

Joy knew he spoke the truth. She joined him in the laughter and her heart filled with happiness and peace for the first time since she'd flown home from New York to take care of things. Everything was done and Joy had nothing to worry about. "I've decided to move back to Minnesota and live right here. Maybe you and I can have dinner or something sometime." She lowered her head, embarrassed.

Pete stood up and walked around the desk. He reached for her arms and gently picked her up. On her tiptoes and him leaning down, he kissed her until she opened her lips as his tongue slipped inside and they kissed passionately for the first time. Then after a moment, he pulled away.

"I'm so thankful to the Lord for all that he's given to me in the past few days. I pray, he'll continue to bless my family as he's done already."

Pete looked at her and smiled. "The Lord works in mysterious ways, Joy. I want to and need to ask you a question. I've loved you for as long as I've remembered, but I've never been sure about your feelings for me."

"I've had a major crush on you since I could remember and after that kiss, well I think I'm even crushing more now than before." She smiled and wiped the lipstick off his lips with her thumb. Then suddenly, she realized how comfortable they were with each other. She was dumbfounded. Looking for the first time really, at his good looks, his dark eyes and short black hair which reminded her he'd been in the service for a few years as a Marine. Now, he'd taken over the spot his father had always held. Driver, butler, grounds keeper and whatever else the estate needed. "What should we do about all these feelings we have and never talked about before?"

"Your father hired my family to manage this entire estate. Joy, your father didn't want you to worry. But I have another important question for you."

She nodded with a smile. "But you didn't answer my question."

"I want to start taking you out on dates. You've always acted as if I didn't exist and now, I have a feeling it was just you being shy? I've always been in love with you. I never thought I would have a chance in hell." He held his hands over his lips. "I'm so sorry, I shouldn't swear."

She giggled. "Pete, really, come on we slip up now and then."

"Anyways, I never thought you would want someone like me?"

Joy shook her head. "I'm a normal person, not anyone special. I'm actually kind of a recluse who'd rather have her nose in a book than be out with friends and party."

"Well, you can imagine how I felt when your dad came over and made me sit down with him outside on the deck." He bounced his leg up and down and seemed nervous.

She giggled and asked, "Oh no, what did my father do?"

"Well, he told me to follow my heart, go to New York and bring you home where you belonged. He said the big Apple wasn't a place for a young lady."

The silence between them was comfortable and for the first time ever, Joy actually felt the love she'd developed for this amazing and special man. The Lord told her many times during church and devotional scripture reading which she'd done daily forever, to trust in him, let go and he would provide.

***

Pete and Joy gathered among their family and friends on Christmas Eve in the big house a few weeks later. They'd decorated in a quick hurry for the holidays. It'd taken a better part of two days with Pete's family and Joy to get it done. She'd sent out the invitations and told everyone to come. Pete's father had already left to go and pick up her dad.

When they arrived, she and Pete greeted her dad and Pete's dad, Peter Senior, at the door.

"Hey, honey." Her dad kissed her cheek. "How are you? The house looks wonderful." He seemed in a good state of mind today. The new group home as well as the doctors had been helpful. They were kind and wonderful for his health, or so it seemed. She didn't take anything for granted with this illness. He had good days and bad days. Today was her father's good day and that was a relief because it would be nice for him to have a great Christmas along with the rest of them.

"Thanks. It took us a lot of work but we got it done." She grabbed a hold of her father's elbow.

"You did me proud daughter. I'm so glad you've chosen to make your home right here. How's the dating prospects going?" Her father laughed.

She was embarrassed but she owed him the truth. "Daddy, Pete and I have nearly spent every moment together. I'm ready to finally admit I'm in love with him and ready to make a commitment, that is if he asks." She turned and smiled at both Pete and his father. "Is that okay with you two?"

"Glad to hear that." Her father patted Pete's dad on the shoulder. "See, Peter, told you I knew Junior, his nickname of Pete since he was a child, and my daughter were a perfect match. You keep that son of yours on the straight and narrow and I'll make sure Joy behaves herself."

Senior took her father over to the table and sat down. They continuously talked together as old friends would. Joy was relieved and glad for both men. It was hard on everyone when her father's state of mind was lost.

After they were seated, Joy looked over at her father who still sat at the head of the table. There were too many people here in her opinion, but it was a tradition and as long as her father was still alive, she was going to make sure she kept those traditions alive.

Joy smiled and raised her glass in the air. "If I can have a moment, please."

The room full of people quieted immediately.

Pete next to her reached under the tablecloth and gripped her hand. Somehow, he knew she needed him.

"I want to make a toast to my father, Dr. Abraham. Although you're retired, you're still an important man in this community. You are one of the best heart surgeons in the United States. But more importantly, I love you, Daddy." She leaned down and kissed his weathered cheek.

The room erupted in cheers and everyone clapped.

After taking a sip of her wine, she set her glass back down then reached down with both hands and squeezed Pete's hands tightly.

He smiled, leaned over and kissed her cheek.

Nobody seemed to notice they were a couple, but Joy knew it wouldn't be long and everyone would know. The two of them had discussed it with his parents and they wanted them to wed sooner than later. It was important to her to have her father walk her down the aisle.

When they'd spent hours on the phone, each had confessed they'd loved each other since high school. That had been at least ten years. Because of them speaking the truth to each other and admitting their feelings, she trusted Pete not to break her heart. She'd assumed before now that he would already have someone in his life, but she found this wasn't true. If he proposed to her tonight in front of everyone, she'd definitely agree.

Everyone was served the first course of the meal by the staff, an apple salad with vinaigrette dressing, her favorite. The guests were busy eating when Pete tapped his knife on his wine glass. He'd chosen to sit next to her and her father near the head of the table which was proper etiquette. Joy wasn't much for the rules but she knew it made her father happy and it was a tradition.

Once the room quieted again, Pete stood up and looked directly at her father. "Dr. Abraham?"

Her father looked up and smiled, "Oh for heaven's call me Dad or my given name, Joseph."

Pete nodded. "Joseph, I'd like your permission to ask your daughter to marry me. I would like your blessing, sir?"

"Well, it's about damn time." Her father pounded his hand on the table.

The people around them chuckled while Pete knelt down next to her chair and picked up her left hand. "Joy, will you do me the honor of accepting my offer of marriage?"

Tears blurred her vision, then a few slipped free and ran down her cheeks. She didn't care as she nodded. "Of course, yes I am honored."

Everyone clapped as Pete stood up, pulled her from her chair and kissed her lightly... They were in front of a lot of people. Their faith in God would always keep them strong. She'd already met with her minister to make sure she did this right. Pete was a very special man and she wanted to do everything in a Christian way. Dating, to marrying then living together in a loving and grateful Christian home. She couldn't marry someone who was lost and didn't have strong beliefs in his faith. She knew with a certainty, Pete agreed with her beliefs and faith. They'd attended the same church since they were toddlers. She enjoyed the people and the minister.

When she asked Pete if he was still happy going to their church, Peach Church, he readily answered her with a 'yes.'

Joy couldn't contain her happiness. It felt as if her heart and mind was finally complete and they'd made a very good decision to get married then start a family. She couldn't help the smile that seemed stuck on her face permanently.

This time, coming home for Christmas had been entirely God's plan for her. Everything seemed to be working out for the best. She prayed to have many years left with her father. For her and Pete to have a blessed marriage and plenty of children.

After she prayed to God, she would let him guide her and give herself to the Lord to do as he may with her. Her parent's faith had always led them in a peaceful and fruitful way. She knew from experience it was a good way to raise a healthy family. Pete's views were the same. They'd discussed many things in the past few days. She found they were still a perfect match as they had been when they were kids. They'd hung out, climbed trees, swam and played together almost every day. They were a perfect fit.

Her father looked over at them, with damp eyes he nodded. "I'm so happy for both of you. Did you get my letter, Joy?"

"I did, Daddy."

"You have no worries here at all. Write all the books you want. I just ask one favor, please?" His brow creased until she nodded, then he smiled. "I want you to write your mother's and my story, please. I would like you to write our story. The tribulations and trials we went through during your young life and illness that nearly killed you. I'd like for you to name the book, *Bringing Joy Home*. Okay?"

She couldn't have figured out a better title if she'd tried. It was perfect. "Of course, Daddy. That will be the next book I write. I love you so much." She leaned over and kissed his cheek. He reached out and pulled her into his strong arms. The Alzheimer's had taken parts of him away from her but his heart and body was still the same.

After she received a hug from her Dad and he'd resumed eating, Pete leaned in and asked her. "Do you have a date in mind?"

She nodded, "I do. How about an April wedding?"

"In four months. Will you have time to plan something that quickly?" Pete asked.

"I've been planning our wedding for the past ten years. Of course, silly, I can plan a wedding in four months." Joy smiled.

Pete threw back his head and let out a boisterous laugh.

She could tell he was immensely happy with his decision to get engaged to her. They'd spent so much time together in the past few weeks and she'd learned a lot about him. They liked the same activities. They both enjoyed sitting in the house, eating a quiet dinner and watching a movie in the living room with the fireplace keeping them warm as they curled up together and enjoyed an evening.

They'd decided to wait for anything further than cuddling and a little kissing until after their marriage. It was something she'd saved for her husband and now glad she had waited.

Joy had found her happiness. Maybe Pete's brother, Patrick, who sat across from her, would find his next. You never know what could happen as long as you keep your faith in God.

"What are you thinking about?" Pete whispered.

She nodded gently towards, Patrick. "Your brother, he seems so sad."

"Oh, you haven't heard?" He frowned.

"No, heard what?"

"Patrick was diagnosed with Bipolar a few months ago. He hasn't been doing good at all. Even his girlfriend Kristy left him, she couldn't handle the mood swings."

"Oh my God, that is so sad. I'm going to start praying for him, okay?"

Pete nodded, leaned over and kissed her cheek. "Joy, you have no idea how much I love you. For you to accept my family as broken as they may be and look at the positive side of things, makes you a very special woman. Thank you."

"Well, I wouldn't expect anything different from you. By the way, I love you, too." Joy kissed his cheek then turned back to the multiple families they had sitting at the table and she noticed one young woman who kept looking over at Pete's brother, Patrick. She wasn't sure who the young lady was but maybe…

The End

A Note from The Author

As a family who had a few elderly members suffer from Alzheimer's it is a terrible disease that takes away from the mind and leaves confusion sometimes in its place. If you'd like to do more research on the disease, you can contact a few places.

The Alzheimer's Association is the world's leading voluntary health organization in Alzheimer's care, support and research.

Alzheimer's is a type of dementia that causes problems with memory, thinking and behavior. Symptoms usually develop slowly and get worse over time, becoming severe enough to interfere with daily tasks.

The most common early symptom is difficulty remembering newly learned information.

Just like the rest of our bodies, our brains chance as we age. Most eventually notice some slowed thinking and occasional problems with remembering certain things. However, serious memory loss, confusion and other major changes in the way our minds work may be a sign that brain cells are failing.

The common early symptom of Alzheimer's is difficulty remembering newly learned information because it typically begins in the part of the brain that affects learning. As Alzheimer's advances through the brain, it leads to increasingly severe symptoms, including disorientation, mood and behavior changes; deepening confusion about events, time and place; unfounded suspicions about family, friends, and professional caregivers; more serious memory loss and behavior changes; with difficulty speaking, swallowing and walking.

If you or one of your loved ones has symptoms, they should seek medical attention immediately. There is medicine that will slow the process down. If you have other questions, contact alz.org. Alzheimer's Association 24/7 Helpline: 1-800-272-3900.

My mother suffers from early stages of dementia and they've actually given her medication to help in the advance. It is nothing to be ashamed of and is no different than any other illness you might be diagnosed with.

With Love
Rhonna Krueger

ABOUT THE AUTHOR

Rhonna Krueger was born in Chisago City, Minnesota and continued her life in the same state. Finding herself retired from her job of almost 20 years, she didn't know what she wanted to do when she grew up. Figuring it out has progressed and her writing is something she enjoys and wants to share. Rhonna is the nickname her Mom and Dad used when she was a little girl and what her mom still calls her. As many of you know her as Rhonda, she will answer to both.

A strong Christian in her faith, she recently found her faith wavering and wasn't quite sure what to do about it. She suffers from multiple mental illnesses and after spending several days in the hospital finally accepting that fact. Realizing how well she relates to many of these illnesses after dealing with them her entire life was an epiphany. She'd been putting her family, children and even pets through the ups and downs of Bipolar and the OCD with the house cleaning to keep everything so perfect and in its place, to locking and rechecking the doors each and every night to make sure of her family's safety.

For the first time in her life, she is ready to share her stories by putting them into fictional characters and stories and even adding based on a true story. Even a small part of the story might be something from her own life growing up and working over the past forty-nine years, but she will bring you to joy, laughter, sadness, grief, fear and eventually happiness. She realized she can relate and create stories around the complex world of the mind and knows how to dance with words as an author can do well. She comes with six years writing experience under a different pen name and another genre. She will be using those creative skills to make these stories shine.

Delivering her soul into each and every contemporary, paranormal, fantasy, military and others such as mystery, suspense and interracial romances, she found herself many times throwing in the God's word or prayer. It might offend many people but at this point in her life she will fight and not be afraid to share her love of God and Christianity to the world. Her decision to become a Christian Romance writer along with women's literature and self-help books stems from her diagnoses and tragic but strengthening injuries bringing her the courage to fight to live each and every day.

Although, she won't tell anyone she doesn't enjoy coming up with a good paranormal or contemporary romance, she needed to add Christian Romance to her real name and wright in her true lane as well as her imagination and creativity life. She wanted to add adversity to her writing profile but under her real name. She is proud of these stories that tell the truth and sometimes are hard facts for people to believe.

She'll still continue with her "day job" of a romance writer but now she's adding to her resume, Christian Romance, Mystery and Suspense along with her Women's Literature and self-help books on living in the moment with mental illness. Some of the material she writes might be too dark for some. In the first couple of pages, she will list what the story entails, the details of her research and the part that is based on a true story. She speaks the truth and writes from her heart. Her family will contest that she is never far from a pen and paper.

If you'd like to contact Rhonna, email her at rhonnakrueger@gmail.com or go to her website rhonnakrueger.com or join her on Facebook.

MISTLETOE MIRACLE
Kristy Johnson

Lake Andrusia - Bemidji, MN

Jenna Otherday turned over in bed for what seemed to be the twentieth time as the tantalizing aroma of frying bacon and brewing coffee wafted into her tiny bedroom. Still tired from the long day of travel, she was hoping to get a few more hours of sleep. It kept eluding her however. All she'd managed to do was toss and turn to avoid the bright light bouncing off the sparkling white snow and into her eyes through the gaps around the window shades. Every cabin she'd ever stayed in seemed to be the same, the blinds never quite kept the light out. It must be an evil plot by cabin owners to ensure guests don't stay too long. After a few late nights and early mornings, people are ready to go home and get some sleep.

The flight from Denver, Colorado had been a piece of cake compared to the drive up from Minneapolis with her parents, Anna and Martin Otherday. Their cabin was ten miles East of Bemidji, Minnesota, putting them in the car for four and a half hours. Her parents had argued the whole way up. The trip had been quite disappointing because she'd been looking forward to spending time alone with them in order to catch up on things. Chaos would erupt when her brother and sisters arrived with their families and she wouldn't have another opportunity to tell them her good news. It had been almost a year since she'd seen them and she was surprised at how much they'd aged. Both of her parents had been very active. They loved the outdoors and had instilled that in their children. All of them hiked, biked, skied, etc. the season never mattered, they found a way to be outside.

We sure had some great adventures growing up.

She sighed, rolled over, sat up, and heard her parents arguing downstairs. She flopped back down on her pillow. "Ugh, it's gonna be a long day if this keeps up."

***

"Anna, be reasonable," Martin pleaded.

"Why do I always have to be reasonable?" Anna huffed slamming the spatula down.

"It's only for a few days. Don't you think this is hard on me too?" He found himself saying. What he really wanted to say was, *please change your mind. I love you. I'm glad we're sharing the same bed this weekend. I want to share it with you for however long we have left on this planet.*

He watched Anna's eyes fill with tears. How did we arrive at this place in our marriage? He felt so helpless. He was waiting for her to lash out again, when Jenna walked into the cozy little kitchen.

"Good Christmas Eve morning you two. How did you sleep?" Jenna asked, breaking the icy chill in the air.

"Fine," Anna responded, turning to get a coffee mug out of the cupboard for Jenna. "Coffee?"

"Yes, please."

Martin extended his cup. "I'd take a little more of that, too, please."

Anna returned the pot to the warmer without refilling his cup and focused her attention on the frying pan.

***

Jenna watched as her father stood there with his mug held out waiting for it to be filled and sadness spreading across his weathered face.

Gathering her courage, she was about to ask what the heck was going on between the two of them when the phone rang.

"I'll get it," Martin said. "Probably one of your sisters, calling to tell us she's running late."

"Smells good, Mom. Can I help?"

"No, I got it under control. You just relax dear. I know you had a rough couple of days."

"Yeah, it's been a busy few days, but I was able to finish my project before I left. So, at least I don't have that hanging over my head."

"That's wonderful dear."

Jenna rested her elbows on the kitchen table, cradling the hot cup of coffee, every so often taking a sip of the hot, rich liquid. She could hear her father talking on the phone in the other room, and surmised it was one of her sisters. No doubt, they were explaining why they were going be late. They were always late. This would be a good time to ask her mother what was going on between her and dad. But how to ask? Instead, she stared out at the frozen lake and admired the spectacular view.

Her parents had once owned a resort here on the Western corner of Lake Andrusia. Unfortunately now, there were only a couple of others left on the lake. What had set their property apart though, was the sixty acres of wilderness that butted into Lake Swenson, a crystal clear spring fed lake with no public access and the harbor out in front of the lodge. Her parents sold it to a developer, keeping a parcel with a spectacular view for themselves. The rest of the land was subdivided into smaller lots and all the owners shared the harbor. Little slips for boats now lined the shoreline where they had fished and ice skated in the winter months. It saddened Jenna to see the development, but she was glad her parents were able to retire on the funds from the sale and she felt grateful they were able to stay on the lake.

She loved the view here, even in the winter. The sparkling monochromatic landscape seemed to stretch forever with the fresh fallen snow over the frozen lake. The sun added sparkle to the frozen crystals of water and cast shadows creating a mysterious depth that forced her to wonder what lie within them. She found peace being Up North. Contentment. Fond memories of growing up here in the wilderness flooded through her brain, making her smile. Then out of the corner of her eye, she saw her mother and her warm memories faded into concern.

For a brief moment, she could've sworn she saw longing on Anna's face as Martin entered the room. He was running his hand through his thick salt and pepper hair, backlit by the sun, his aging but muscular body, was still a sight to see. A display not lost on

Anna, Jenna thought. It was creepy to think about your parents in this way, but on the other hand, Jenna felt happy there still might be hope for her parents.

"They're all running late as usual," Martin announced.

"What excuse did they give this time?" snipped Anna.

Martin, wincing at his wife's tone, paused before answering, "You know, the usual stuff."

Jenna jumped in before either one could continue the frosty conversation, "I'm sure they'll do their best to get here before church."

Martin and Anna maintained eye contact for a moment longer before Anna returned to her meal preparations and Martin retreated to the office.

It's gonna be a long day, if I don't do something.

"Mom, how about we go cross country skiing after breakfast?"

Anna didn't respond.

"Mom?"

"Yeah. Sure. That sounds nice, Jenna."

***

Large fluffy snowflakes gently fell on Jenna's nose as she clicked the toes of her boots into her cross-country skis. She felt as if she were suddenly plopped into a giant snow globe.

Beautiful.

"Are you ready for this, Mom?"

"You betcha."

"Sure you don't want to join us, Dad?"

"No, I need to run the plow over the driveway and clear the sidewalk before your brother and sisters get here. You two go have fun."

Disappointment? Relief? Jenna couldn't quite tell what emotion was written on her parent's faces. She really needed to get to the bottom of what their issue was or this was gonna be a really long week. "All right, we'll be back in a couple of hours."

"Sounds good. I'll be here." Martin stood there and watched

them go.

Jenna peeked back a few times, not only to make sure her mother was keeping up with her, but because she wanted to see if her father was still watching them.

He was.

She was barely able to make out his form, but he still stood there. Something really bad must have happened between the two of them to cause them to be so angry with each other. They'd been married for thirty-six years and Jenna couldn't even remember them having a single fight or any type of disagreement. They'd always treated each other with respect and kindness. Maybe one of her siblings knew what was going on. She'd been so preoccupied with her job that she hadn't been paying much attention to her parents the last few months.

Change was coming though.

"Jenna. Jenna. Jenna, Stop!"

Jenna came to an abrupt halt. She'd been so absorbed in her thoughts she must have kicked it into over drive. Looking back, she could see her mother several blocks behind her, struggling to catch up. Jenna, an avid outdoorswoman and used to the mountains, wasn't even breathing hard. She planted her poles into the snow, and grabbed her water bottle out of her waist pack as she waited for her mother to catch up.

"What's the hurry, honey?" Anna asked, gliding up next to Jenna.

"Sorry, Mom. I guess I just got into a groove and started going."

"That happens." Anna laughed.

"Yeah, I guess it does."

Jenna smiled. Her mother looked more relaxed and kind of happy for the first time since they picked her up from the airport. It was nice to see. "It's so peaceful out here. I forget how different it is from Colorado. While there is a majestic beauty in the mountains, there's a calm peaceful beauty here on the lake."

Following her daughter's gaze around the lake, she nodded her head in agreement. "Well, we'd better start heading back. The snow is picking up and it's getting dark."

Before Jenna could ask about what was going on between her parents, Anna took off in the direction of home. Jenna easily caught up with her mother and they'd only traveled a short distance when the soft white flakes turned into angry ice pellets in the swirling wind. The temperature also plummeted and they shivered despite their exertion. They weren't dressed for artic weather, they were dressed in cross-country ski attire, which was made for aerobic activity not cold bitter winds.

Heads down, they battled the snow and wind for what seemed like at least an hour to Jenna. They were in white out conditions and could easily get separated in the raging storm. She was getting worried. They should be getting close to home.

Anna stopped abruptly.

"What is it, Mom?" Jenna shouted over the raging wind.

"I'm afraid we've veered off course in the snow."

"We're lost?"

"No, we aren't lost, we just passed our mark."

Jenna looked around confused. She couldn't see a thing. "Are you sure?"

"Yes, Jenna. I'm sure. I've lived on this lake nearly my whole life and I think I would know my own shoreline."

"Well, we'll just turn around then."

"No, it's too late for that now. I think we need to find shelter."

"Shelter? But who's around this time of year?"

"Well, I thought the Larson's said they were coming up for the Christmas holiday and I am pretty sure that's their cabin up ahead."

Jenna looked to where her mother was pointing with her ski pole. Way up in the distance, she could barely make out a small orange glow emanating out of the darkness. "Are you sure it's their cabin?"

"Pretty sure. Doesn't matter though, we need to get out of this storm. Just keep focused on that light, head straight towards it."

"Okay, right behind you Mom."

Step and glide. Step and glide. They kept a steady pace through blizzard right up to the Larson's backdoor. They were really off course. The women had passed their house and ended up on the North side of the lake. Good thing the Larson's had a phone, so they could call and let Dad know where to come find them. No one would ever guess this was where they were.

They quickly unlatched their skis, leaned them against the thick log siding and then knocked on the door as loudly as they could. The door slowly opened revealing a bare chested Seth Larson. Jenna nearly gasped at the sight of this fine male specimen in front of her. The warm glow of the orange fire lit up his glistening skin, defining well-formed muscles. She looked him over, taking him in ever so slowly, his biceps, his chest, the small little area between his belly button and belt buckle. A moment of desire quickly passed over her and turned to horror as she realized her mother stood behind her, watching her drool over this man that once was her biggest crush. They'd stolen a few kisses when they were younger, but then he went off to college and the fledgling romance ended.

"What are you two doing out on a night like this?" he asked startled by the sight of the two frozen women.

Anna glanced at Jenna quizzically, then answered, "We were out cross country skiing and got caught out in this storm. Can I use your phone to call Martin?"

"Phone's out," he responded still gaping at Jenna.

"Well, could you give us a ride then?" Jenna asked, finally finding her voice.

"I'd be glad to if we weren't snowed in. I just came in from trying to clear the driveway. Plow hasn't been by yet."

"Your father is gonna be so worried," Anna muttered.

"I know Mom, but there's nothing we can do. We can't go back out on the lake."

"No, you can't," Seth said. "Why don't you ladies come in and sit by the fire. Get warmed up. There's no power. My folks were going to stop at the store on the way up, but they're not here, so I'm assuming they are snowed in somewhere. Not sure what there is to eat, I'm afraid I only brought a few granola bars up with me."

Jenna smiled. "I'm sure whatever you have will be fine. Right now, the big thing is we need to call my dad, he's really going to be worried about us."

"I wish I could help with that." Seth nodded. "But as I said, the phone is out and my cell is totally dead."

"I really need to let Martin know where we are."

"There's nothing we can do, Mom."

"He'll understand."

"No, I don't think he will."

"I'm sure he will, Mrs. Otherday. Now come, sit by the fire and warm up."

"I guess you kids are right," Anna said, resigning herself to the situation. "Your Father is gonna be just beside himself."

They sat on the couch in front of the raging fire and started shedding some of their wet outer clothing. Jenna was soaked to the bone with sweat, but no way was she taking off her clothes in front of Seth. He'd seen enough when they were teenagers.

He came back into the room, arms laden with blankets and assorted pieces of clothing. He donned a nice red flannel shirt. It was untucked and he had left the top three buttons undone.

Casual.

Relaxed.

Sexy.

What is wrong with me? My mother is sitting right here next to me and I'm having these less than pure thoughts about a man I haven't seen in years.

"I dug out some of my mom's clothes for you, Mrs. Otherday. Jenna, I didn't see anything of hers that I thought would fit you. You're so much taller than she is, so I brought you some of my clothes. I hope that's okay."

"That's very sweet of you. I'm sure they'll be fine."

His clothes. She wanted to hold them up to her face and breathe them in.

Stop it!

"Thank you Seth. Your mother would be so proud of you for thinking of us."

"No problem, Mrs. Otherday."

"Please call me Anna."

"Okay, Anna."

"Now, if you'll excuse me, I'm going to go get into some dry clothes before I freeze to death," Anna said, heading down the hall to the bathroom.

Seth and Jenna stood there in the center of the room in awkward silence for a few moments before speaking in unison.

"So, how…?"

This made them both laugh as the discomfort of seeing each other again, faded away and they both relaxed.

"So, how have you been?" he asked.

"I'm good. You?"

"Good." He smiled.

"Your turn," Anna broke in.

"I won't be long. Then you can tell me what you've been up to." Jenna winked and headed down the hall.

He watched her go.

Anna stood and watched them both.

Jenna ventured a peak and turned around; she saw a wistful look upon her mother's face.

And the desire on his.

Upon closing the bathroom door, she leaned her back against it and brought his little bundle of clothes up to her face. She inhaled deeply.

Clean.

Fresh.

He'd brought her clean clothes.

She was just being silly now.

She let out a small sigh and slowly began the process of peeling out of her wet things. She grabbed a wash cloth out of the linen closet and hoped there was enough pressure in the reserve tank that she could at least freshen up a little bit for him.

For him? Ugh, I have to stop this. He's seen me in worse shape. When we were kids.

She did the best she could to make herself presentable before exiting the bathroom and heading back towards the warmth of the fire, and Seth.

"No cell phone service either?" Anna asked.

"Nope. Phone is down. Roads blocked. We are just gonna have to ride out the storm."

"Just figures, the biggest blizzard in twenty years hits and its Christmas Eve," Anna complained.

Jenna wrapped her arms around her mother's shoulders. "It's going to be okay, Mom."

"I know. I'm just worried about your brother, sisters and of course, you're Dad. He's gonna be so worried about us."

"I know, but there's nothing we can do. We're stuck here for a while."

Anna started pacing.

"That's not going to help, Mom. Try to relax."

"Relax? I can't relax. Your Dad and I, well we've never not known where the other was before. He's will be frantic."

"He'll understand, Mom. He'll know it wasn't your fault."

"She's right Mrs.—I mean Anna. Everything will be all right."

"I don't know," Anna said, continuing to wear out the living room carpet.

Seth and Jenna exchanged a look of concern.

"Why don't we see if we can wrangle up something to eat? I'm sure you ladies are hungry."

Jenna watched her mom do a few more laps before she calmly walked over to her and gently grabbed her arm, ushering her towards the kitchen.

"Come on Mom, let's go see what we can find to eat, you need to keep up your strength."

"You're right." She allowed Jenna to usher her towards the kitchen.

Walking side by side with her mother, there wasn't much room to pass into the kitchen.

Seth moved aside to let them pass, smiling at Jenna as they did. He looked relieved..

She returned his smile as they passed, her free arm gently brushing across his midsection.

The proximity was electric.

He smelled of pine, and wood smoke, with a gentle hint of cologne.

Inviting.

Masculine.

Definitely all male.

Jenna quickly moved past him and into the inviting little room. She didn't want to, she wanted to lean into him, to linger there.

Stop it! Your mother is standing right next to you. Not the time.

"Oh, good it's a gas stove. We'll be able to have a hot meal," Anna proclaimed as she began to work on preparing an edible meal.

Jenna sensing her mother was grateful for the distraction, settled onto one of the barstools at the island counter.

Seth followed her lead.

The three of them made idle chatter while Anna cooked. They talked about where they were living, work, and things they liked to do for fun...Purposely avoiding any mention of Martin and the rest of the family. The conversation flowed, it wasn't forced, and there were no awkward pauses. It felt comfortable, just like the little cabin. Seth made frequent trips to add logs to the fire since they couldn't afford to let it die out.

"Well, it's not gourmet, but it's hot," Anna announced after about thirty minutes of commotion in the kitchen. "Jenna, set the table please."

"Sure thing, Mom. Seth, which cupboard are your plates in?"

"Dishes and silverware are to the left of the sink, cup and mugs to the right."

"Thanks."

"No, thank you." With that, he left to go put another log on the fire.

"He sure turned out to be a handsome young man, don't you think so Jenna?"

"Mom," came an embarrassed reply.

"I may be old and married, but that doesn't make me blind to a nice piece of man candy."

"Mom!"

"What? Can't I speak the truth?"

"I'm shocked. What would Dad say?"

"Unfortunately, not much."

"What do you mean by that?"

"Oh, nothing dear."

"Come on, Mom. You and Dad have been at each other since I got here. What's going on?"

"Nothing you need to concern yourself with, dear."

"Mom, I love you and Dad, you *are* my concern."

"Not now, sweetie."

"If not now, Mom, then when?"

Anna stared at her daughter.

Jenna stared back. She wasn't going to let this go.

Anna's lower lip quivered and her eyes filled with tears, but she still didn't speak.

Jenna said nothing, just patiently waited for her mother to continue.

Anna opened her mouth to speak, then closed it, repeated the process, then turned away when Seth entered the room.

"Everything okay in here?"

"Just fine," Anna replied.

Seth looked at Jenna, then Anna, and then back at Jenna.

Jenna shrugged.

"Sit, Seth," Anna commanded.

"Yes, ma'am."

The carefree manner in which they'd been conversing earlier was now gone. They sat in silence. Jenna desperately wanted to continue their conversation. She couldn't imagine what was going on between her parents. She felt she'd been close to getting her mother to open up about the situation going on at home. If only Seth had come in just a few moments later, her mother might have opened up.

Seth.

She glanced up to see him watching her. She felt her face get hot. She could either look at Seth, who made her blush or her mother who made her worry. She chose her mother.

It was safer choice.

"Mom, you look tired."

"I must admit, I am. Been quite a day. Seth, do you have a place where I can lay down for a bit?"

"Yeah, sure, let me show you."

They left the room.

Jenna put her spoon down and rested her face in her hands. It had been quite a day. She should've been exhausted. She looked up startled when Seth touched her shoulder.

"You okay?"

"Yes, thank you."

"Why don't you go rest by the fire, I'll clean up."

"Thanks, but I'll help. It will go quicker."

"You really don't need to."

"I know, but you've been so kind."

"Aww, couldn't throw you back out in the storm, it wouldn't be neighborly," he said winking.

She smiled.

He smiled back.

Clean up consisted of scraping the plates, emptying out the liquids and stacking the dishes neatly by the sink. Not much else they could have done without water and they didn't want to melt any more snow. They returned to the living room and piled a few more logs in the fireplace then took up residence on opposite sides of the couch.

"So, you live in Colorado?"

"Yes, I've been there for about five years now."

"Do you like it?"

"I love it there. The mountains are absolutely amazing, I'm just really far away from my family."

"I know what you mean. I've been in Seattle for the last five years."

"Really? What have you been doing out there?"

"I had a startup company that revolved around 3-D printing."

"Sounds interesting."

"It was."

"What do you mean was?"

"I just sold it, I'll be moving back here."

"You are?"

"Yep. As of last week, I am officially homeless. That's why I'm here at the cabin. My folks said I could stay here while I look for a place to live."

"That's really nice."

"It is. I'll be able to catch up with them and make sure they're managing okay."

Silence.

Jenna had stopped talking and was, staring down at the quilt she was under. She fussed with a loose thread, keeping her hands busy while she organized her thoughts.

He waited.

She kept staring at the quilt.

"You want to talk about it?" Seth asked politely.

Jenna got up, threw a log in the fire and began pacing like her mother had hours before.

He watched her.

Finally, she began, "I arrived the day before yesterday. I was so excited to get here and see my family. I had just finished a really big project, which was such a huge relief."

"Is that what you were talking about earlier?"

"Yes. It went so well, that I've been given a big promotion. I'm being to be transferred to Minneapolis."

"That's wonderful."

"I know. Right?"

"Are your folks excited you're moving back?"

She was still moving about the room like a caged animal. Back and forth. "That's the thing, I haven't been able to tell them."

"Why not?"

"Because every time I start to tell them, they start fighting. The only reason Mom and I left the cabin today was because I thought a little separation might do them some good."

"That's not good."

"I agree. I'm so worried."

Seth got up to put another log on the fire.

Jenna watched him as he bent over to pick up a log and throw it in the fire.

What a beautiful backside. Mm-mm.

He turned, and faced her, the flames flickered wildly behind him, just like the flicker of desire burning inside her soul for this man whom she hadn't seen in years.

Just like old times.

She resumed her pacing, lest she linger on his perfect form any longer.

"So, are you going to talk with them about it?" he asked as he stepped towards her.

"Yes. Though, I'm thinking I might talk with my brother and sisters first. Maybe they know what's going on."

Stepping closer, he said, "Sounds like a good idea."

"You don't think they're going to get a divorce do you?"

He stepped closer still. "Your parents?"

She changed her path. "Yes, my parents."

Seth changed his trajectory to match hers, closing the gap between them even more. "No, I don't think they'll get divorced. They love each other too much."

Jenna changed direction again.

He matched her step.

She stopped moving. "How can you be so sure?" she asked watching him approach.

Grinning at her, he came closer.

Jenna didn't move. She maintained her position and waited for his response.

It didn't come.

He stopped directly in front of her.

She wasn't sure she liked the look on his face. It was that impish grin that boys get when they are about to do something naughty.

Seth smiled.

Nervously, she smiled back at him.

He didn't move.

She could smell him now. Fresh pine and wood smoke.

He smelled good.

"What?" Jenna asked nervously.

A wry grin spread across his face as he lifted his eyes up to the ceiling.

She followed his gaze.

Mistletoe!

She looked back at him. His grin was bigger now and he was quickly closing the small gap between them.

With a gasp, she attempted to move back.

He reached out and grabbed her waist pulling her in close. "Oh no, you don't. It's tradition."

"My mother."

"She's sleeping."

She opened her mouth to protest again, but she was silenced by the warmth of his lips on hers. They were soft and warm, sensual. He kissed her softly at first, tentatively, gently wrapping his arms around her pulling her tight against him. Jenna stood rigid. She did not resist him, though she didn't kiss him back.

Seth persisted.

It paid off.

Slowly, ever so slowly, she moved her arms up around his back embracing him. She parted her lips allowing him in deeper.

He did not squander the invitation.

She let out a small moan as his tongue touched hers. He had hit the ignition switch and she was now kissing him back—hard. She let her nails sink into his back.

Seth pulled her in tight, kissing her fiercely.

She could feel his passion.

And his desire.

She was slowly coming back to her senses, regaining control. Moving her hands from his back to his chest, palms gently resting on his firm pecs she gently pushed him backwards, separating their lips as she did so.

He kissed her again, gentle this time, then rested his forehead on hers, their breathing slowly returning to normal. "Because they love each other."

"What?" Jenna asked, opening her eyes to look at him.

"Your parents, they won't get divorced, they love each other too much. I think they've just gotten caught up in something neither knows how to end. They'll get through it, I'm sure of it."

"I'm glad you're sure, because I'm not."

With one hand resting on her hip, the other gently stroked the back of her head coming to rest on the back of her neck. He pulled her close bending his head to hers, kissing her again. This kiss wasn't one of passion, but one of reassurance.

"It will be. Now quit fretting." Removing his hand from her hip he glided it up to her elbow, then to her wrist and finally to her hand as he pulled her back to the couch.

***

Anna, groggy from her restless night's sleep, crept quietly into the hall. She stopped before entering the sitting area, and smiled.

Ashes and glowing embers were all that remained of the fiery blaze Jenna and Seth had kept going during the night to keep them all warm in the little cabin.

On the couch lay her daughter, sleeping peacefully, head in Seth's lap, with her long dark hair cascading around her shoulders. Seth, his blonde hair tousled, was leaning back on the couch with one hand gently resting on Jenna's shoulder. They were a handsome couple. Jenna, half Ojibwa and Seth one hundred percent Norwegian, complemented each other. Anna always liked Seth and had been happy when the pair had dated back in high school. She didn't know what transpired to end their relationship, but was glad to see them back together.

Anna remained motionless in the hall for several moments, staring at her daughter allowing her senses to wake up. She could hear the drone of a snowmobile somewhere in the distance.

Life.

There was life somewhere out in the frozen white world outside of the cabin. The sound drew her attention to the little kitchen window above the old cast iron sink. That's when she saw it, the yellow-green flash of the microwave clock. It flashed, 12:00, 12:00, 12:00. *The power was back on!* Hopefully, it meant the phone was back on also. She could call Martin. Where was the phone in this place? And began looking around for it.

Spotting the phone, she headed over to it. So focused on making a phone call, she hadn't heard any other sounds and was startled by the front door crashing open just as her hand touched the receiver.

"Aahh," Anna gave a startled cry, knocking over the phone, startling Seth and Jenna awake.

Both bolted to their feet in time to see Paul and Sheila Larson, feet covered in snow, being shoved aside by a frantic Martin Otherday. "You're here!" He cried relief clearly visible on his face.

"Oh, Martin," Anna proclaimed running to her husband, leaving the phone bouncing down onto the old oak floor.

The couple embraced, momentarily forgetting their anger towards each other. Then as if they remembered they were supposed to be angry with each other, they let go.

Disappointment darkened Anna's face as she looked at Martin, but she kept her tone in check and simply asked, "Are you okay?"

"Yes, I'm fine. You? Jenna?"

"Yes, we're both good. It was a godsend that Seth was here."

Martin located Seth in the tiny room, his eyes narrowed a bit at the sight of Jenna. Her back was pressed into Seth's front and his arms were wrapped around her, and she was clasping her hands around his. "Thank you, Seth."

"You're welcome," he replied playfully.

Jenna caught his tone and cocked her head to look at him.

He was staring directly above her mother and father's heads. She followed his gaze.

They were under the mistletoe.

"Umm, Mom, Dad?"

"Yes, Jenna?" Anna asked.

"You do know its tradition, right?"

"What's tradition?" Martin asked.

"To kiss when you're under the mistletoe," Seth replied, still smirking.

Martin and Anna both peered up to gaze upon the mistletoe, then at each other. Permission was granted with their eyes and they kissed. Their bodies relaxed as all was forgiven.

Anna was the first to pull away, but she stayed close and whispered in Martin's ear so only he could hear, "I am so sorry, I'm not sure how we arrived at this place, but I love you and want to spend the rest of my life with you. That is if you'll still have me?"

"I will always *have you* my dear. I love you, too. Will you forgive me?"

"Oh yes Martin. I do."

He kissed her again then whispered in her ear, "Merry Christmas, my love."

"Merry Christmas, my love," she whispered back as tears of joy filled her eyes.

***

Jenna's eyes filled with tears watching her parents make up for whatever had transpired between them.

Seth seemed to sense her relief. He pulled her in tighter and speaking softly into her ear, "I told you they'd work through it."

"Yes, you did." She squeezed his hands.

Seth nuzzled her neck a little more sending little shock waves down her spine as his hot breath caressed her skin. He planted a small kiss at the base of her neck, before whispering into her ear, "Merry Christmas, my love."

Still in his arms, Jenna turned to him and stared deep into his eyes. "Merry Christmas." Then she kissed him.

ABOUT THE AUTHOR

Kristy Johnson received a degree in Chemistry and Biology from Bemidji State University. Growing up in Bemidji, Minnesota, she now resides in Jordan, Minnesota with her husband, two boys, two dogs, and twelve chickens. *Mistletoe Miracle* is Kristy's fifth short story to be published in a group anthology and she is working hard to have her first full novel published in 2017.

When not writing, Kristy can be found exploring Minnesota or taking photos. Her company, Fotonic Images, LLC specializes in portrait, real estate and fine art photography.

To learn more about Kristy, her adventures or her publications, you can follow her at:

www.WildhorsePublications.com
www.facebook.com/WildhorsePublications
www.amazon.com/author/KristyJohnson
www.twitter.com/FotonicImages
www.FotonicImages.com
www.facebook.com/FotonicImages

NAUGHTY AND NICE
Kathleen Nordstrom

Crystal Lake - Burnsville, MN

"Frances Lee Allen, stop bugging me about when you and your sister Chloe can go see Santa."

"But, Mom, you promised we could go after Thanksgiving," Franny whined while kicking off her snow boots.

"After Thanksgiving! We just left Grandma and Grandpa's house after celebrating Thanksgiving. Tomorrow, you can write your letters to Santa."

"Mom."

Don't Mom me, young lady. Get upstairs and get ready for bed." Sallee held Chloe tight in her arms as the sleepy child rubbed her eyes. "Go back to sleep, sweetheart. It's late and past your bedtime."

Once both Sallee's daughters were tucked into bed, she went back downstairs to the kitchen. Opening the fridge, she took out an opened bottle of Zinfandel. "Shit, I forgot the leftovers in the car," she said out loud. Taking a glass out of the cupboard, she muttered, "Who cares, the girls hate reheated lumpy mashed potatoes and mushy green bean salad leftover from Thanksgiving dinner anyway." As she poured the chilled liquid into a glass, her phone rang. "Hello," she answered it. "Hi, David. Yes, we had a nice time at my parent's house. All my side of the family was there. Yeah, both my sisters showed up. How was your day with your family in Wisconsin?"

"The meal was fine." His deep voice came over the line. "My family wanted to know how my law firm was doing. My mother asked me about you and when were we getting married."

"What did you tell her?" Sallee asked quietly looking over her wine glass before taking a large sip.

"I told her we hadn't talked about it yet."

"Oh." After a few quiet seconds, Sallee asked, "How did the rest of the day go?"

"Well, my Harvard sister, bickered most of the afternoon with my older sister the Berkley lawyer, over politics," David replied sounding annoyed. "Then my mother—"

"Wait, stop!" Sallee interrupted him. "I just poured myself a glass of wine. Why don't you come over? We can commiserate about our day together?"

"That sounds like a great idea," David agreed.

"Okay, see you soon. When you get here, I'll make you forget all about your sisters."

Thirty minutes later, dressed in a chenille bathrobe, Sallee opened her front door, before David could ring the doorbell.

He kissed her hello.

Wrapping her arms around his waist, she kissed him right back. She pulled him into her house by his belt.

He folded her inside his cashmere overcoat, while he kicked the front door closed.

She led him by his belt into the den to the left of the front hallway and just off of the living room. Opening her chenille robe exposing her naked body to him, she said, "This is for you."

"Damn, woman! You'll catch your death of a cold undressed like this."

"Build a fire," Sallee coyly suggested. Once he built a cozy warm fire in the fireplace, she said, "Have a glass of wine." She held up a filled glass for him, she had poured for him on the fireplace mantle.

"Dammit, Sallee, You're killing me here." He rubbed his erection.

"Wine first. I'm a glass ahead of you."

He took a sip with a pained look on his face. "Sorry, I can't." He put the glass on the coffee table.

She dropped her robe, standing naked in front of him while he quickly dropped his pants. Stepping out of them as they collapsed on the couch and facing the fire. Continuing their kissing, Sallee rolled him off the couch onto the floor giggling. "Shush. Don't wake my girls." She snickered, feeling like a teenager afraid of getting caught. But that didn't stop her from making mad passionate love with

David.

"That felt like angry sex," David said sitting up after he rolled away from her, wiping his brow with the back of his hand. "Like I said earlier, Sallee, you're killing me."

She poured them more wine, while still sitting on the floor; she leaned up against the couch.

He got dressed, picked up her robe and gave it to her. "You'd better put your robe on in case your girls wake up." He sat on the floor next to her, took a big gulp of wine, and pushed back his black curly hair drooping over his forehead. He leaned back on the cushion. "You first...tell me about your day."

"I pretty much gave you the highlights on the phone. The girls had fun with their cousins playing outside making a snowman. Then they complained about not being able to ice skate on Crystal Lake in my parent's backyard. It wasn't frozen hard enough."

"There must have been more going on," he prodded.

"Well, yes. The first thing out of my sister Janet's mouth was, 'Where's that gorgeous lawyer boyfriend of yours.'"

"Oh, she thinks I'm gorgeous?" David winked at her.

"Stop it, David. Of course you're gorgeous." Sallee nudged his shoulder playfully. "My sister bitched about her job being so demanding, leaving her very little time for herself. The whole time my two sisters and I were in the kitchen helping with dinner, my mother went on and on, coming up with suggestions for how my sister could cut back and make time to do the things she wanted to do."

"That was nice of her," David joked.

"Nice? Are you kidding me?" Sallee poked him in the arm.

"Ouch. I'm not the enemy here."

"Enemy! Janet is arrogant, condescending and doesn't understand why I don't get a better paying job. I asked her what's wrong with being a hotel food services manager. I almost blew a gasket listening to her. What the hell does she know about having no free time? She's not married and never has been, has no kids, was valedictorian in high school and college. She makes over $200,000 a year with plenty of perks and bonuses, drives a new Jag that's paid for. The woman owns a million dollar house with a gardener and live-in housekeeper who keeps her house immaculate and a damn cook to make her meals regardless what time she wants to eat. Oh, and I forgot, she has a pool she never swims in. A damn pool! I've never been invited to swim in her pool."

"Sallee, take a breath," David urged and put his arms around her preventing her arms from flailing around.

"Well, David, there's more."

"More?"

"My sister just ticked me off with her tirade about her life. She knows this time of year is hard for me."

"I know it was right before Thanksgiving, four years ago when your husband was killed by a drunk driver," he said.

"Anyway, she kept carping about enough time had passed since Brad's death and you and I should get married."

"We should you know," David whispered.

"I know, but…stop changing the subject," Sallee protested. "She also reminded me that Chloe was only a few months old, at the time of his death, so she doesn't remember him. Then she added that Franny was about four years old, so she probably doesn't remember much about him either. My sister just ticked me off with her tirade about her life. Then her judging mine, too."

David wiped a stray tear from Sallee's cheek. "She just knows how to push your buttons." He hugged her.

After a few minutes, she calmed down. "I feel stupid. Let me go," she said quietly.

"I will if you'll behave."

Sallee sighed deeply. "I will, I promise."

He held her glass to her lips. "Take a drink of your wine." David pushed her blonde hair back from her face, tucking her long tresses behind her ears. "Did you spout off like this at your parent's house?"

"No. I stormed out of the house and went down by the lake

then screamed bloody murder in the boathouse. I punched a few holes in several of the extra Styrofoam rose bush covers my father stores in there."

"You didn't. Did you really do that?" David tried to hold back a laugh.

She nodded at him over her wine glass.

David put his hand up to his mouth trying to smother his snickers.

"I'll have to call my dad tomorrow and tell him what I did." She looked at him with raised eyebrows and a smirk.

They laughed heartily together.

"There's never a dull moment with you, Sallee," he said kissing her forehead.

"Anyway, the ride back home from my parent's house was also stressful."

"My God, doesn't this drama ever end?" He leaned over and gazed into her tear filled eyes.

She snuggled closer to him, sighing deeply; as she took another gulp of wine and continued, "With the girls getting older it gets harder each year. Franny kept bugging me, wanting to know when they could go see Santa. She said she had to see him right away to tell him what she wanted for Christmas. I questioned her about what was so urgent. All she said was she wanted to make sure he had enough time to find her a present."

"So what did you tell her?"

"I told her to write Santa a letter and if she didn't stop bugging me about going to see Santa, she'd get onions and potatoes in her stocking."

"Sallee, that's awful," David scooted closer. "Please tell me you didn't say that to her."

"Yes, I did."

"Why?"

"David, I'm not sure Franny still believes in Santa. So why does she want to go see him?"

"Does Chloe believe in Santa?"

"I'm sure she does, honey."

"Maybe Franny is just trying to keep up her belief in Santa for Chloe."

"Oh, David. Maybe you're right." Sallee snuggled into his chest, while he stroked her hair.

"Well, we'll just have to make things right with the girls and tell them you were stressed out and didn't mean what you said," he suggested.

"I am exhausted. I need a good night's sleep."

"That's a good idea. Let's go to bed." He helped Sallee stand up.

"Not tonight." She stopped him with both hands on his chest. "I need a good night's rest."

"Come on, Sallee. You said it yourself this time of year is so lonely," he protested.

"I know, but with you in my bed, I know I won't get any sleep."

"Oh, baby, you know me too well." He kissed the top of her head and gave her a long bear hug before leaving.

***

The following morning Sallee woke with a headache. Wine hangovers were the worst. Thank God, she had the day off. Sitting on the edge of the bed, trying to fully wake up, she could hear her girls talking downstairs. After splashing her face with water in her bathroom, she dragged herself downstairs to the kitchen.

The girls stopped talking when Sallee walked into the room.

"Good morning, girls," she greeted, trying to be cheerful while her temples throbbed. She kissed each of them.

Chloe smiled up at her from her chair at the table. "Mommy, look what I did. I wrote my letter to Santa." She beamed.

Sallee looked over the letter containing random letters written in red and green crayon. She had drawn colorful ornaments and blue snowflakes on the page also. "It's beautiful, Honey."

"Franny helped me spell some of the words."

"That was nice of her to help you," Sallee commented looking at

Franny who sat across the table from Chloe. "Thanks for helping your sister, Franny."

"Sure Mom," Franny said quietly, folding her own letter to Santa before putting it into an envelope. "Chloe, do you want to mail your letter in the same envelope as mine?" Franny asked as she showed Chloe her envelope.

"Okay," Chloe said beaming.

Franny added Chloe's letter inside her envelope and sealed it. She addressed it to Santa Claus, North Pole, USA. "Mom do you have a stamp?"

"No, but I can take it to the post office and get the correct postage. Can I do it later this afternoon? Look, girls. I'm really sorry I was so crabby and mean to you last night. I'll make it up to you with a day at the mall of shopping and you two can see Santa."

"When?" Chloe asked excitedly blurted out.

"I'll let you know, okay?" Sallee said rubbing her temples. "Right now, I really don't feel well. In fact, I have to go back to bed for a while."

***

"I just checked on Mom and she's sleeping. Come on, Chloe, help me look."

"For what?"

"Don't you want to know what Mom got us for Christmas?"

Chloe shook her little head sideways while she gave Franny a big, sweet, angelic look. "How do you know the presents are here at home?"

"I heard mom talking to Grandma yesterday and Mom said she had all her shopping done."

"What if they're already wrapped when we find them?" Chloe asked Franny.

"We'll be careful and open one end, so we can see what's inside and then we'll tape it back up." Franny jumped up and grabbed Chloe's hand then dragged her out of their room. "I think I know where they are."

They went upstairs to the attic.

Chloe started tugging to get away. "We're not supposed to be up here. We'll get spanked."

"Stop being such a baby. No one will know."

"I will," Chloe said.

"You know what I'll do if you tell? I'll tell Mom it was your idea because you're such a baby and couldn't wait for Christmas. Now shut up!" Franny had taken down the big skeleton key she knew was in her Dad's old beer stein on the top shelf of the china hutch in the dining room.

Chloe socked Fanny's arm. "You'll get a spanking. You're not supposed to be in the attic. You're going to get it."

Franny glared at her. "Remember what I told you?" Franny slowly opened the door to the stairs leading up to the attic. When they got to the top of the stairs, there was another door. Franny stuck the key into the door. The key wouldn't turn in the lock, she kept trying to turn it— until the key broke in half, leaving the broken part still in the lock.

"Now you've done it," Chloe said and raced back downstairs to their bedroom.

As fast as Franny could, she put what was left of the key back in the beer stein and went to their bedroom.

***

Three days after breaking the key to the attic door, Franny and Chloe were playing dolls, having a tea party in their room, when their mother appeared in the doorway. Without a sound, she held up the broken key and gave them the look—the one raised eyebrow—that said your life was over. Sallee saw the fear on their faces. She didn't say anything for a few minutes. "What happened to this key? What were you doing in the attic?" she snapped.

Franny froze. She didn't take her eyes off the broken key.

"I'm waiting. Frances Lee what do you know about this?"

Chloe started to cry and put her small hands over her face.

Sallee gave Franny the look again.

"Ah—ummm." Franny swallowed noticeably. "Well…" She swallowed again. "We…" She shuffled her feet. "We were looking for our swimming suits," Franny blurted out.

Sallee blinked her eyes shut and tilted her head back in disbelief. She sighed heavily.

Franny hung her head.

"Swimming suits in December?" Sallee started to laugh. Then she left her daughters alone and went downstairs to the kitchen to call David. "David, are you busy right now? I need you. I'm the most horrible mother in the world. Can you please come over?"

"Sallee, what's wrong? Stop crying. I'll be right there."

When Sallee opened the door to let David in, he wrapped his warm arms around her. "*Shhh*, whatever it is we can fix it. I'm here. Don't cry." He kissed her hair and rubbed her back. "Come on, honey, let's sit in the kitchen and you can tell me all about it. I know you love the holidays. This is our third Christmas together and you've never been like this before at the holidays. Are you feeling well? Maybe you need to see a doctor."

"Maybe I should. I've been so tired and exhausted these days," she agreed and took a deep breath.

They sat in silence for a few minutes.

Finally she spoke, "I know you're right. What I need right now is to lie down. My head is pounding."

"Look, Sallee. Why don't I take the girls for the day, so you can get some rest?"

"Oh, David, that would be wonderful."

"Mommy, are you all right?" Franny asked as she and Chloe walked into the kitchen hand in hand.

"Oh, Franny, yes sweetie pie, I'm okay."

Both the girls hugged her.

"Great, now all three of you are crying. You're going to make me cry," David said. He stood up and went to the sink to get a glass of water. "Turning from the sink facing the girls, he said, "Girls, get dressed. The three of us are going out and have some fun. Who wants to go to the mall?"

"What about Mommy?" Chloe asked looking sad, still hugging her neck.

"She's going to stay home and rest, so she will be all better by the time we get home."

He winked at the girls.

***

"You two can eat anything you want," David said as the three of them entered the Burnsville mall food court.

"Can we have ice cream cones, David?" Chloe asked.

"Like I said, anything you want."

"Do you know my mom said we couldn't see Santa yet?" Franny looked like she was going to cry.

"Yes, she told me."

"Let's go have those ice cream cones."

After they ordered and sat, he prompted them, "Finish your ice cream and we'll go see Santa."

"David, can we really? You're the best," Franny said bursting with excitement. "Come on, Chloe, we have to get in line. Let's go." Almost pulling Chloe's arm out of its socket.

David stood in line with the girls holding their coats, hats and mittens for about thirty minutes. Chloe acted a little timid, so he stood close behind her while she shyly talked to Santa.

Franny was next. She wasn't afraid at all. Santa looked surprised when she told Santa what she wanted. She whispered it to him with her hand cupped to his ear. When she was done whispering, she leaned back and put her hands together like she was praying, with a pleading look on her face.

"Come on, David, get in the picture with us and Santa," Chloe and Franny pleaded.

"Mom's gunna love this picture." Franny beamed.

"Speaking of your mom, do either of you know what she wants for Christmas?"

"She wants to be happy," Chloe said shyly.

David smiled. "What would you like for Christmas, Chloe?"

"Nothing. We've been bad." She motioned for David to lean down to her. She whispered in his ear, "I know what Franny wants. She wants a daddy."

David stood up. "Really? Are you sure?"

Chloe nodded her head like a bobble-head doll.

"Chloe, never mind," Franny scolded as she jerked Chloe's hand and started walking fast. "David, can we have some of those little corn dogs at the root beer place?" Franny asked politely.

"Sure. Let's go. Do you want a float with that?"

After they ate again, David treated them to a movie.

Several hours later, he brought two sleepy girls home to their mother. Chloe had fallen asleep during the third, one hour animated Christmas movie. Franny had fallen asleep in the car, on the ride home.

Sallee waited in the living room while David carried them one at a time upstairs and put them to bed, clothes and all, not wanting to wake them.

"So how was your day?" Sallee asked when David sat down on the couch next to her.

"Where do your girls get all that energy? I'm surprised they're not sick after eating ice cream, root beer floats, mini corn dogs, popcorn and chocolate covered raisins. The mall theater had a special on one hour animated Christmas movies. I'm exhausted. How do you do it all by yourself?"

"Some days, I wonder."

"Someday, I'd like to be a father, but not a single one." He kissed Sallee and gave her a hug. "You look better." He kissed her nose. "Did you get any sleep?"

"A few good hours after tossing and turning for two hours, after you left."

"Do you want to talk about what happened earlier Sallee?"

"What happened? I had a headache. Now, I just want a hug and to cuddle."

"I want you to know I plan to buy the girls special Christmas gifts."

"David, I love you," Sallee said.

**

A few weeks later on Christmas morning, Franny and Chloe got up at the crack of dawn. They crept downstairs, entered the living room and found their mother asleep on the couch. There were the two gifts they had put under the tree for their mom and David along with several other wrapped packages. Chloe took her small hand in Franny's and led her to where they had hung up their Christmas stockings on the mantle. They eagerly took the bulging stockings down and dumped out their contents on the floor, only to find they had been filled with onions and potatoes, but there was a note attached to each sock.

The note read:

Dear Franny and Chloe,

I'm sorry to put these vegetables in your stockings, but you did disobey your Mom.

You can always use them in a pot roast.

Love, Santa

Sallee sat up on the couch startling the girls and she noticed they were laughing with tears in their eyes. "Stop, wait," Sallee said stopping the girls from going back upstairs to their room. She got off the couch and hugged her girls. "Let me go make coffee and then we can open our presents."

While the coffee brewed, she looked at the girl's stockings and their contents on the floor. Her heart ached for doing this to them, but she felt they needed to be taught a lesson. David was pretty steamed with her for going through with her threat. Now more than ever, she wished she hadn't done it. The house was extremely quiet, so she turned on the radio to a station playing Christmas music. "Franny, will you turn on the lights on the tree."

Franny beamed. "Sure, Mom." When she went around the side of the tree to plug in the lights she saw a package from Santa with her name on it.

"Okay, girls. I've got my coffee and I'm ready to open presents." Sallee sat on the couch and the girls sat on the floor in front of the tree. "Franny, you can pass them out."

"Here, Mom, open ours to you first." Chloe squealed as she handed her a small package that looked like a four year old had wrapped it.

"Oh my, what can this be?" Sallee carefully opened the box, setting the ribbon aside and smoothing out the wrapping paper before folding it neatly.

"Come on, Mommy, open it!" Chloe clapped her hands.

"Chloe, this is beautiful." She held up a ceramic handprint of Chloe's right hand, which, Chloe had painted blue. Sallee hugged Chloe and kissed her cheeks all over.

"Mom, you're going to break me."

"Okay, Mom. Now, open mine," Franny said excitedly.

Sallee started the same procedure opening her present as she had used on Chloe's gift.

"Come on, Mom. Forget about saving the paper and open my gift," Franny protested.

Inside the box was a necklace made of colored wooden beads strung on a large round shoelace.

Sallee put the necklace on and jumped up to look at herself in the big mirror above the mantle. "Franny, this is beautiful. I'm going to wear it today."

"Okay, get the boxes wrapped in red, Franny. They're from me," Sallee said.

The girls tore into their red packages. "A new dress!" Chloe crowed and held it up.

"I got a new pair of black patent leather shoes," Franny exclaimed putting them on.

"Wow, I got new shoes too, just like yours, Franny." Chloe held up one shoe.

"I got a new dress too, just like yours, Chloe."

"You two can wear your new red and green, plaid taffeta dresses with your new shoes to grandma's today and I'll wear my new necklace."

"Mom, there's more presents under the tree," Franny said timidly.

"Well, go ahead and see who they're for," Salle urged with a big grin.

"Mom, Mom, they're from Santa!" The two girls didn't waste any time ripping open the packages.

"Show me what you got," Sallee said excitedly.

Chloe dumped out her box full of at least two dozen rubber duckies of all themes. "I love these duckies!" She beamed.

"What did you get, Franny?" Sallee asked.

"Look, Mom, it's the complete set of Nancy Drew books. I never asked Santa for these."

"Well, the day is not over yet girls."

Franny already had her face buried in volume one. After breakfast, she and Chloe dressed in their new Christmas dresses and shoes.

Sallee combed and put bows in their hair that matched their dresses. Then she hugged Chloe hard.

"Ouch, Mommy.

"Oh, sweetie pie, I'm so sorry," Sallee said, barely able to talk. "I'm just so happy."

***

All the cousins were at grandmas. There must have been thirty or so relatives.

Sallee kissed her parents, hugged as many relatives as she could before putting her desserts in her mother's fridge.

"Where's David?" Sallee's dad asked.

"I'm not sure he will make it today, Dad," she replied while doing the busy work of helping her mother set up the food, buffet style.

A knock sounded at the back door.

"Hello, David. Come on in. Let me take your coat." Sallee heard her father welcoming David to the party.

David went straight for the Christmas tree. He emptied a large red Santa bag full of gifts next to the tree. Ignoring everyone, he swiftly went into the dining room, straight over to Sallee. "Hi, honey." He kissed and nuzzled her neck. "Beautiful necklace."

"Did you have anything to do with this?" she asked David.

"I'll never tell. Where are the girls?"

Her father handed David a glass of wine, which he set down at the table.

"Franny, Chloe," he shouted over the din of the festivities.

Everyone stopped what they were doing and stared at David.

"Franny, Chloe, come here. I have something for you two."

"David. What are you doing? You're making a scene. You're embarrassing me." Sallee tried to grab his arm.

He moved out of her grasp, kissed her cheek and whispered in her ear, "Honey, I want to give your girls their Christmas presents from me now, since I can't stay long," he said loud enough for all to hear.

Just then, the girls appeared at the top of the stairs.

"Come on down, girls," David commanded. "I have something for you two."

The girls eagerly ran down the stairs.

"Come on over here." David pointed to two large wrapped packages. "Go ahead." He prompted putting one present in front of each of them.

Chloe giggled and clapped her hands as David helped her take out a large doll that stood almost as tall as Chloe. "Here now, open this one," David said and put another gift in front of her. Inside were several outfits for her new doll, along with several other accessories.

"Franny, it's your turn." David gave her a box not as big as Chloe's.

"Mom, look. It's an iPad." Franny held it up, so all could see.

"Here's another gift for you, from me." David helped Franny

open a box full of books.

"Thank you, David." Both girls hugged him at the same time, kissing him on his cheeks through tears.

"David, you're the best," Franny whispered to him.

Chloe nodded and said, "The very best."

"I have to leave, but I hope you all have a very merry Christmas and enjoy your meal." He winked at Sallee before he disappeared out the back door.

"Sallee, what a great guy you have there," her sister, Janet said while giving her a quick hug.

Her girls hugged and kissed her, too.

She couldn't stop the tears from rolling down her cheeks.

"Mommy, what did David give you for Christmas?" Chloe asked.

Sallee pulled Chloe onto her lap. "Sweetie pie, he didn't give me anything yet."

"Why," Chloe persisted.

"Maybe later."

"Time for dinner," Grandma announced.

Plates clatter, people chattered, kids laughed and giggled as they filled their plates.

"Listen up," Sallee's father interrupted as he banged on a saucepan lid. "Time to say grace."

Once they all prayed, the chatter continued as everyone enjoyed the wonderful meal.

When it was about time for dessert, Sallee's dad made an announcement, "David had to leave early but he left a gift in the garage for Sallee. Let's all go out there to see what he gave her." Her father grinned.

In the garage was a cardboard box the size of a refrigerator.

"What is it?"

"Open it up, you ninny," Janet yelled pushing her to the front of the box.

The box wasn't wrapped but was tied with a wide ribbon and

had a large bow on top.

"Dad, give her some scissors."

As soon as she cut the bow and ribbon off the box, David popped out of it, dressed in a Santa suit.

"Oh, my God!" Sallee shouted, holding her chest as if she was having a heart attack.

David knelt down on one knee and opened a ring box with a beautiful diamond in it. "Will you marry me?"

"Yes," she peeped as her eyes widened. "Yes, yes, yes!" She grabbed him and buried her face in his neck.

Her family and guests broke into a round of applause.

David released her from their embrace and presented her with the ring.

"Put it on me," she told him. They embraced again.

Her family cheered and clapped.

"Who helped him with this?" Sallee asked the crowd.

Almost everyone shook their heads, except her dad and sister. "Dad, Janet, what do you have to say for yourselves?'

"Well, David asked me to help him get into the box. It wasn't easy finding a box to fit his six-foot four frame into," her dad explained pointing to the box. "Thank God, I found an appliance store that still uses refrigerator boxes."

A round of laughter erupted.

"Janet, what part did you play in this?"

"Remember Thanksgiving, when you and I helped mom with the dishes? You left your opal ring on the sink before you stormed outside. That's when I measured it, or I actually traced it on a paper towel for David."

"You rat." She nudged David in the ribs.

"He asked me to find out what your ring size was," Janet said with a huge grin.

"This calls for champagne," her dad announced.

They all went back into the dining room. Her mother lined up all the glassed she had on the table while David brought in a case of champagne from the garage. Corks popped and when all the adult glasses were filled, and the children along with Sallee, had a glass of coke. They all stood still for a toast.

"I want to wish David and Sallee a life of happiness and love. I know you will be a great father to Franny and Chloe. Cheers and welcome to the family." Her father lifted his glass and he took a sip.

They all raised their glasses and someone yelled, "Welcome." They all drank and toasted David and Sallee.

During the merry making, Sallee pulled David outside onto the back porch. "David, I love you so much. I apologize for being so crabby. I'm actually embarrassed to admit how wonderful you've been to my girls. I don't have your gift."

"I know what you can get me, Honey. A son."

Sallee started to laugh. "What if it's a daughter?"

"Well, that would be okay I guess."

"You guess? You take whatever we get. Well, personally I don't want to know until the baby is born. I want to be surprised."

David just stood staring blindly into Sallee's eyes.

"David. Are you all right?"

"Are you telling me I'm going to be a daddy?"

"Yes."

"Are you sure?"

"Yes. The doctor confirmed it yesterday."

"Whoo-hoo! This has turned out to be the best Christmas ever," David shouted.

ABOUT THE AUTHOR

Kathleen Nordstrom is a native of Minnesota and now lives in Burnsville. She is married, no children of her own, but her husband has two grown children and two grandchildren.

She received a two-year AA-Liberal Arts degree from Normandale College, Minnesota, where she graduated with a Phi Theta Kappa designation. Continuing with her undergraduate education, she received her Bachelor of Arts degree from Metropolitan State University, Minnesota with a major in Business and a minor in Creative Writing.

Kathleen is a co-founder of Romancing the Lakes Writers Chapter of Romance Writers of America® which was established in 2012. She writes Romantic Mysteries of the Cozy type with no blood and guts gory murders, or explicit sex, but always has a dead person and an amateur sleuth.

Visit her at: http://kathleennordstrombooks.blogspot.com

OLD YULE LOG FIRES
Rose Marie Meuwissen

Lake Minnetonka - Excelsior, MN

Old Log Theater
City of Excelsior

"I said no interruptions, Molly. I have to get these ads in by ten or we won't have any advertisements for this last minute *Christmas Time Again* show, that for some reason, Mike thought we could fit in!" Tara Knutsen glanced up from the file on her desk and leaned back in her chair with exasperation reeling from every inch of her trim body.

"I know, I'm sorry, but he's here." Molly fidgeted her fingers into an iron fist in front of her body while she waited for a response.

"And just who is here, that has you in such a tizzy?" Tara stared at Molly, wondering if the whole world was against her getting this ad submitted this morning.

"The lead actor for the Christmas show."

"Now? He wasn't supposed to be here until tomorrow night!"

"Yes, but he's here now. What should I tell him?" Molly shuffled her feet back and forth in a rocking motion.

"Well, I can't talk to him right now. If I don't run these ads, there won't be anyone at his little impromptu last minute show." Tara spun her chair around to face the window to see the snow coming down gently. For now, anyway. A snowstorm was forecast for later in the afternoon, and probably why he flew in early. *What else could possibly go wrong today?* "Tell him I'm on a conference call and will be out to meet him in about thirty minutes."

"Sure. What if he doesn't want to wait? After all, he's a big movie star and they can be kind of –you know what I mean."

"Take him on a tour of the theater and by the time you're done, I should be ready." Tara made a shooing motion with her hand for Molly to leave and refocused on the file she'd attempted to open only minutes before.

She hadn't even had time to read it yet, much less get the advertising ready. Mike plopped the file on her desk a few minutes after she'd arrived in the office this morning. Just who was this guy that he had the nerve to show up a day early and expect her to be available? She opened the file and flipped through the papers to the back sheet to find his name and photo.

When she looked at the man's extremely photogenic face in the picture, her breath caught in her chest. His chiseled features, strong jawline and jet black hair brought back memories she'd buried long ago. She didn't have to look at the name to know who he was, she would know those dark brown eyes anywhere. They were the eyes that haunted her dreams for the past ten years. She could feel her blood pressure rising at the thought of seeing him again. He'd changed his name, she knew this much, but she hadn't cared to find out what it was. Now she knew. Tyler Callaghan was now Ty Logan. And apparently, he waited just beyond her door. She felt literally sick. *Maybe I could plead a migraine and leave before they came back?*

Tara had little choice at this point. She needed to do her job and face her worst nightmare. Hell, they were *only* high school sweethearts. Never got engaged. They were only kids back then and had no idea where their lives were going or where they'd end up. Unfortunately, she'd assumed they had a future together. He'd been her first love and she thought he loved her, too. Then he'd left and never contacted her again. Obviously, he hadn't felt the same about her. She'd hoped to never see him again, but deep down she'd believed this day would come.

The advertising was taken care of and it had only been twenty minutes. Just enough time to Google *Ty Logan. Did that mean a person was famous if they had their own Wikipedia page?* Well, he did have one and it said he'd done some B movies and been in a few TV shows. She did feel a little surprised to find out he'd been singing for fun at some events, recently. Apparently, she wasn't the only one who liked to listen to him sing. *After living in LA all these years, why would he want to come to Minnesota and sing at the Old Log Theater on Lake Minnetonka?*

Being an adult, Tara knew she would live through coming face-to-face with her ex-boyfriend. But damn it, she was still pissed as hell at him, and definitely didn't have to like it. Perhaps she could act like she didn't know who he was? Yeah, maybe she could give that a try.

After a few deep cleansing breaths, she rose slowly from her chair and walked to the door. Another deep breath and she opened it. For a moment, she hesitated, when she saw him turn her way.

Briefly, an elated expression crossed his tan chiseled face. Yes, this was one very hot, sexy man. Quickly, he walked towards her extending his hand to shake hers. Now with a much more serious expression, his eyes locked on hers as if he was trying to see deep into her soul. "TJ Sandstrom," Tyler stated and waited patiently for her response.

Of course, he would use her nickname and maiden name. "Tara Knutsen," she corrected him and extended her hand to meet his, but as soon as their hands touched, it became overwhelmingly apparent the shocking chemistry they'd experienced as teenagers was still there. "Mr. Logan, welcome to the Old Log Theater. I hope you enjoyed your tour and Molly filled you in on what will be happening for your show."

"Yes, she did. Thank you." Tyler released her hand slowly.

"Please let the stage manager, Tom, know if you need anything. If you are all set then, I need to get back to work." She waited for his nod to say she could end this meeting, but it was slow coming.

"I'm good, for now, but can we discuss some small details concerning the show and its advertising over dinner? Say tonight, if you're free?"

"I have plans for tonight." Her nerves were raw. *How dare he ask me to dinner at the last minute and expect me to be free?*

Mike, the theater manager, walked over to where they were standing just in time to hear her decline Tyler's invitation. "Mr. Logan, I'm sure Tara will be happy to rearrange her schedule to accommodate your gracious offer for dinner." He gave her a stern look.

"Of course, Mr. Logan. If it's important and can't wait until tomorrow, I can cancel my plans."

"Lord Fletcher's at seven, then. Would you like me to pick you up or would you rather meet me there?" Tyler asked.

"I'll meet you there." With the inevitable settled, she turned and walked back to her office, shutting the door gently behind her, even though she very much wanted to slam it. *Hell yes, I'm driving myself!* It would only be a short quick dinner and then she was leaving.

Promptly at seven, Tara pulled up to Lord Fletcher's restaurant and used the valet service. She got out of her SUV and with her manicured nails, she nervously straightened her form fitting low cut black dress which fell mid-thigh. Then she pulled her long black wool coat closed. Her goal, of course, was to show him what he'd passed up for Hollywood.

***

Tyler waited patiently in the lobby. As soon as he saw her long legs in knee high black leather boots with her hot sexy body in a short, skin tight dress walking provocatively through the doors, he knew it was his TJ. He could sense the unease she'd felt at seeing him again and she had every right to be mad. His heart had skipped a beat when he first saw her today.

Her long reddish blonde hair fell gently past her shoulders and her big blue eyes were like pools of clear blue lake water totally mesmerizing him. She'd appeared to be even more beautiful now than when they were in high school, if that was even possible. He'd been a fool back then. Leaving her behind had always been his biggest regret. He loved her and no one else ever came close to making him feel the things she did. If it were possible to correct a mistake he'd made ten years ago, he intended to do it.

He immediately walked over to greet her. Unexpectedly, he leaned in and pulled her towards him for a kiss, wrapping her tightly in his arms. To his surprise, she responded by kissing him back. Pissing her off wasn't what he had in mind though, so he reluctantly stopped. He smiled at her and motioned towards the door. "I'm sure our table is ready."

Turning away quickly, Tara entered the restaurant.

"Do you have a reservation, sir?" the hostess asked.

"Yes, Ty Logan," he quickly answered.

"Right this way." The hostess escorted them to a deep burgundy rounded booth with high leather-like backs providing some privacy.

"Please bring us a bottle of your house wine," Ty stated.

"Certainly." The hostess left swiftly, seeming to be eager to do his bidding.

"I'm grateful you accepted my offer for dinner." Tyler intently watched Tara's face, waiting for her reaction, while the hostess returned with their wine and filled each glass.

Tara twisted her glass, then took a sip as she stared at him intently. "I didn't really have a choice."

"Everyone always has choices. We can all only hope we make the right ones."

"Apparently, you did," Tara retorted implying what they both knew was his decision to leave years ago.

"Is that the way it appears to you?" He never felt nervous but talking to her tonight was one of the hardest things he'd ever done. This was the woman he loved and he'd broken her heart years ago.

"Yes." That was all she said, but her eyes were a force to be reckoned with almost as if she was daring him to deny it.

"It may look that way to you, but I'm not sure." He'd wanted to go to Hollywood and become a famous actor. Unfortunately, he'd felt he needed to do it alone, so here they were basically strangers after all these years, trying to get past the pain and hurt his decision had caused.

"Is that why we're here? Did you expect to find me married with children? A fat, dumpy housewife? Is that what you were hoping?"

"Actually, I was hoping to find you still as beautiful as ever."

"Really? And just sitting around waiting for you to return?"

"Well, I knew that would be asking a lot, but yes something like that. And may I say, for the record, you are even more beautiful today than when I last saw you."

Thank heavens the waitress appeared at the table just in the nick of time. After placing their orders, they both sat staring at each other.

Finally, Tara broke the silence, "I think we need to change the subject to work related. I looked over the plans for your show and was surprised to learn you would be doing a musical Christmas show."

"You, of all people know how much I like to sing. Even after achieving success as an actor, what I really wanted to do was sing. Only after I became somewhat well known, would they allow me to perform songs on the shows. So doing this live show is really something I've wanted to do for a long time."

"I always loved to listen to your singing."

"I figured if anyone would let me sing on their stage, it would be in my home town. So I had my agent contact the Old Log Theater and here we are."

"I'm sure it will be a great show."

The waitress brought their bread and salads as they discussed the show. Lord Fletcher's was known for their steaks and seafood and once the dinner plates were served, it left no doubt as to why.

After they'd finished their dinners, he requested a dessert menu. "We'll take the Mud Pie," Tyler informed the waitress without asking Tara's opinion. He wondered if she remembered this was the same place they went to dinner for Prom. Mud Pie was what they had for dessert. "I wonder if it's still as good as it was?"

Tara stared at him. "I guess we'll find out. The last time I was here was for Prom with you."

***

As soon as dessert was done, Tara got up to leave but he insisted on walking her out. "Thanks for dinner," she said as he moved closer to her. Out of the corner of her eye, she could see other women, even those with men, ogling Tyler. She knew he was famous but she didn't need anyone taking pictures of her with him and printing it in the newspapers or tabloids. He was her past and that would be the way it would stay. Heck, women were probably throwing themselves at him all the time. He definitely wasn't going to be kissing her again, either. So as soon as the car pulled up, she walked around, got in and left him standing there without another word.

While she drove away, she could see him still standing at the curb. She had to admit, it wasn't so much that he might try to kiss her again, it was that she just didn't trust herself not to kiss him back.

Why did he have to come back now? And to my theater? She truly never expected to see him again. It had taken five years to get over him and during those years, she'd really thought he would come back. But he didn't. After meeting Steve, she tried desperately to fall in love with him and even thought she had. So she married him, hoping then she would experience the same feelings for him that she'd felt for Tyler. Sadly, it hadn't happened. Three years later, the divorce papers were filed.

When she looked Tyler up on the internet, it showed pictures of him with many different women. They were all gorgeous and obviously, he could have any of them. *Why was he really in Minneapolis?* She didn't have a clue but she needed to stay as far away from him as possible because the only thing that could come out of this situation was for her to get her heart broken again.

The next week went by quickly and she hadn't seen him too much since he was rehearsing the show like a mad man to get it perfect. She tried to avoid being where he might be as much as possible. Saturday, December 12–tomorrow–the first show would open and it would run for ten days with the last show just two days before Christmas Eve.

Every time she walked by the theater and he was singing, she stopped to listen. He'd always been a great singer, in fact probably a better singer than actor. Of course, she wasn't going to tell him that.

Needless to say, it was going to be a spectacular show and they were sold out for all ten nights.

Evergreen boughs hung from the ceilings, pine wreaths decorated the walls along with red and white Christmas lights. In the main foyer, a nine-foot spruce Christmas tree stood with red and gold ribbon bows, white lights and ornaments hand made by the Old Log employees. Mistletoe hung over the main door, only it was hidden–not noticeable among the other greenery and flowers–so unless you were extremely observant or actually looking for it, you wouldn't see it.

It had been snowing again and she decided to head out early to do some Christmas shopping when accidentally she ran right smack into Tyler's chest as she came around the corner.

"Easy does it, sweetheart." His lips were inches from her cheek.

"So sorry," she said and quickly backed away. When their bodies touched briefly, she felt sparks like she'd never felt before. She couldn't help wondering what it would be like to feel his hard body pressed against hers while having wild crazy sex.

"Where are you off to in such a hurry?"

"Oh, just wanted to get in some Christmas shopping before the weather gets too bad."

"Living in California, you forget about the dangers of driving in snow."

"It'll probably come back to you."

"Care if I tag along with you? I'd love to have some company for dinner. Never liked eating dinner alone."

"Tyler, what do you want from me?"

"Ever wonder what would've happen if I'd stayed?"

"You didn't, so it doesn't matter, does it?"

"That depends."

"On what?" She was getting agitated now. Of course, she wondered, why wouldn't she?

The rest of the show crew came walking down the hall towards them, laughing and talking.

"I'll buy," Tyler offered, deliberately avoiding her question and gave her his sexy grin that usually had women falling at his feet.

"Fine, let's go," Tara finally said as she didn't want to deal with the rest of show crew.

He followed her out to the parking lot. The snow had been falling steadily all afternoon, leaving about two inches of fresh snow on the ground.

"Where's your car?" she asked.

Tyler pointed to a shiny new Chevy Suburban still sporting dealer plates.

They continued walking to her SUV, a Christmas red Ford Escape. He immediately picked up the snow scraper from the backseat and brushed it off while she started the engine. Minutes later, she drove to downtown Wayzata and parked. It was dark now and the streets were lined with Christmas lights and decorations.

She loved Christmas! And this was why. Everything was decorated so beautifully.

Tyler got out, came around to her side to open the door and helped her out.

It'd been years since she'd spent any time around Christmas with a man. Unfortunately, only a temporary situation though, and she needed to keep telling herself this because he would be leaving again. Maybe for a little while she could just enjoy her time with him. As a friend. *Hell, who am I kidding?* They were more than friends back then. She'd given him her virginity long ago on Prom night. The chemistry between them had been strong then and it hadn't died out even one bit—like a smoldering old log fire that hadn't gone out completely. The attraction they felt could easily be fanned into a brilliant burning flame once again.

Together, they strolled down the sidewalk in front of the Main Street storefronts. She went in the shops where she saw interesting items in the windows and he followed with a smile.

"I thought guys hated to go shopping."

"I'm thoroughly enjoying this. Interesting, quaint little shops.

I'm glad they've kept this area alive and vibrant all these years. It must be a nice place to live."

"They've done a good job, I agree. I especially like to come here at least one time before Christmas."

While they walked along Main Street, they ultimately ended up at what once was *Sunsetter's* for many years, now under new management and called *Cove*. Large wreaths with large round red glass bulbs adorned the front doors.

"The new restaurant looks welcoming and warm. Want to have dinner, here?" he asked.

"I don't—know," she replied eyeing the doors.

"It's only dinner. You must be hungry."

"Okay." After all, she'd only had a snack for lunch. How difficult could it be to have dinner with him, again? In fact, she might actually enjoy it. So far, he'd been good company and he *had* initially invited her to dinner.

Apparently, someone on the staff recognized him, because they got the best table in the place, on second floor directly overlooking Lake Minnetonka and Main Street. Once seated at their secluded table, they weren't bothered by other people dining who might have realized a celebrity dined in their midst.

They ordered the special, Salmon, and opted for just coffee since it was still snowing and the roads would be slippery.

"I have to say, I miss this little town. So tell me what you've been doing all these years?"

"Going to college, getting a job, etc. The usual stuff."

"Did you leave out getting married?"

"I would think that was obvious by my last name."

"I don't see a ring."

"Divorced. It didn't work out. How about you?"

"Never took the big step. Didn't think it would work out with anyone I'd met."

The rest of the conversation centered around small talk and about how Wayzata had changed over the last years. After finishing their meals, they managed to make it out of the restaurant without being stopped by any over-anxious fans. The snow seemed to be coming down pretty good by then, but she made it safely back to the Old Log Theater to drop him off.

It was nearly ten when she pulled up beside his SUV, now covered in snow.

Tyler pulled out his key and pressed the auto start button. "Thank you for letting me tag along for your Christmas shopping night in Wayzata and for rescuing me from having to eat dinner alone."

"I had a nice time. Thanks for the dinner and the company."

Tyler jumped out, and opened the door to pull out a snow brush and begin the task of clearing off his vehicle for the drive home as she drove away.

***

Opening night was a huge success, with rave reviews being printed in the local newspapers. Tara had sat in the back row of the theater to watch the show, telling herself it was part of her job, but she really wanted to see the show. The man was good, she would give him that and damn good looking, too. Even though he'd only been back a short time, she could tell she was falling in love with him all over again. *That is if I ever stopped loving him.*

The ten days of the show went by quickly and each night, they had a full house. Once it ended its run, he would most likely be leaving and heading back to Los Angeles. Every time she saw him at the theater, he smiled at her and he always acted gracious and kind to the staff. Never once had she seen him act haughtily towards anyone. *Could he still be the nice guy I once knew and fell in love with? Do I dare tell him I still have feelings for him?*

Finally, the last day of the show arrived and Molly walked into Tara's office carrying a flyer. "There's a party at Ty's tomorrow night for the staff," she said and handed one to Tara. "Everyone's excited to go see his house. You're going to go, aren't you?"

"Of course, if everyone is going. I wasn't aware he had a house in Minnesota. Where is it?"

"Someone said it's a huge mansion on Lake Minnetonka. Gotta hand all these out, so I'll be back in a little bit."

**

Tara's SUV turned up the long winding driveway to Tyler's place. The large brick house loomed in front of her. Every window glowed from a single candle and the house had been completely trimmed with white lights. She still couldn't believe this was Tyler's. *Why would he buy a mansion on the lake when he lived in California?*

Getting out of her SUV, she heard, *Jingle Bell Rock,* emanating from the open door as several people entered the beautifully decorated house. Through the large front window, a Christmas tree, ornately adorned and totally aglow from the multitude of white lights, could be seen. Inside, people dressed in their holiday finery conversed and laughed while enjoying each other's company.

When she reached the door to knock politely before letting herself in, it opened and Tyler greeted her with his sexy and stunning smile. "Tara. Glad you made it." He stepped aside, so she could enter. While she unhooked her coat, he waited to take it. "Let me put your coat away, for you."

She waited patiently until he returned while taking in the center staircase adorned in evergreen boughs and red ribbons. *Blue Christmas* played in the background. It seemed like such a happy place and it gave her a comfortable feeling. She smiled at him when he returned and took his arm as he extended it to her.

"Let me show you my new house."

He showed her each room on the main floor and then proceeded upstairs to show her the master bedroom. Molly had been right, this was definitely a mansion! The bedroom looked enormous, complete with a sitting room, exercise room, massive his and her closets and a large veranda outside of the triple patio doors. She didn't know what to say. "It's absolutely gorgeous. Who will you be sharing this bed with?" she asked pointing to the large king bed. As soon as she asked, she wished she hadn't.

"That depends on what happens here."

Sheer shock overtook her. "What does that mean? You want to have sex here and right now?"

"Not exactly, but by no means would I turn down a chance to make love to you again." He laughed softly.

"What do you want from me, Tyler?" She had no idea what might be happening or was about to happen.

He moved closer and wrapped his arms around her. "I never stopped loving you, Tara. I would like a second chance for us." His voice lowered and his lips moved closer to hers until they touched her waiting lips. This time, he kissed her not holding anything back— like he never wanted to let her go again.

Her resolve to stay guarded, melted away and she kissed him back with every ounce of her being.

Tara thought about the huge inviting bed behind them, but knew she wouldn't be using it tonight. Reluctantly, she moved slightly away from him to end the kiss, even though every inch of her body wanted him inside her. "This is happening too fast, Tyler," she whispered to him. "I was mad at you for way too many years, so I couldn't even move on. I waited for five years, hoping you would come back for me, but you didn't."

"But after that, you got married, right? So you did move on."

"I tried to, regrettably I never loved him the way I loved you. I had to let him go, so he'd have a chance to find a love like you and I had. Unfortunately, I don't think I ever stopped loving you, which left me unable to love anyone else."

"I never married because I never had feelings for anyone else that even came close to what I'd felt for you. That's why I came back home. For you."

"And you bought this house, why? Are you staying in Minnesota?"

"I want to take some time off from Hollywood and get back to my roots. Hopefully, get married and start a family. With you."

Tara backed away, running her fingers through her long reddish blonde hair. "This is really a lot to take in, Tyler. I've waited for ten years to hear you say those words, but now that you finally have, I don't know what to say."

"You don't have to give me an answer tonight. I've been thinking about this for the past year before making my decision to come back home and contact you. It was sheer coincidence that you were working at the Old Log. Or maybe it was fate. Our fate."

"Tyler, this is ten years later. We are older and we are different people now than we were before. Getting back together may be a dream come true for us, but we need to take some time and really get to know each other again."

"I've got time. I'm willing to go slow if that's what you want. I would just like a chance to find out if we still love each other enough to make it work. The Ordway offered me the lead in their new play, so I'll be staying here for a while."

"I need to take some time to think about this. It really has been quite a shock to hear this from you."

"I'm alright with that." He took her in his arms and softly kissed her cheek. Then brushed her lips gently with his, before kissing her once again. Slowly. Almost as though he was afraid it could be the last time he would have the opportunity.

She ended the kiss and laid her head on his shoulder. Not wanting to let go either.

"You do realize the chemistry between us is off the charts?" Tyler whispered in her ear.

"I do." Tara couldn't believe she was actually thinking maybe they should be moving to the bed only inches away.

"I have every confidence we can make it work and have a long and loving relationship."

"We probably should go mingle with your guests," Tara suggested, knowing this wasn't the proper time to take this any further.

"I'd rather not, but you're probably right, we should." He hesitated a moment, then took her hand in his and they descended the stairs to join the party.

The food he had catered in was top notch and she thoroughly enjoyed it while conversing with her co-workers. She watched Tyler out of the corner of her eye as he also mingled with the guests.

Finally, ten o'clock came and people were making their way to the door to head home. After all, tomorrow was still a work day for them even though the show had ended.

Tara ended up being the last to leave, but not because she planned it that way. She'd already remotely started her car and had it warming up, when she realized everyone was gone and only she and Tyler were left standing in the foyer.

Tyler brought her coat out and helped her put it on. She suddenly felt tempted to ascend those stairs with him and use that welcoming king bed where they could become reacquainted with each other, but it was late. She had no doubt in her mind that every inch of her being wanted to be with him, but she really needed to think about this with a clear head and in the light of day.

"Would you like to spend Christmas Eve together?" Tyler asked. "We could make dinner here."

"I go to church on Christmas Eve, would you like to join me?"

"I'd love to. You still go to Grace Lutheran?"

"Yes. I can pick you up at five-thirty. Afterwards, we can cook dinner." Tara felt excited at the idea.

"Great. I'll go grocery shopping tomorrow morning."

Tara leaned into him and gave him a quick kiss. Then turned and walked to her car. She could feel his eyes on her back, watching her walk away from him and she smiled.

***

On Christmas Eve morning, Tara woke to bright sunlight streaming in through the small opening at the bottom of her curtained window.

She hadn't been this happy at Christmas time in years. It'd been lonely spending it by herself. On Christmas Day, she always went to her parent's house for dinner along with her sister, brother and their spouses. Neither had children yet, so it was strictly an adult's Christmas. She hadn't allowed herself to even think about what it would be like with children or a husband since there wasn't anyone she'd been serious about since the divorce. Did she dare think about it now? Was he being honest about his intentions? Should she take the chance to find out? Hell, if she knew whether it would work out or not. The only thing she had to lose by trying would be her heart. Again.

After showering and dressing, she headed out to find the perfect present for Tyler. She didn't know of course, if he would be getting one for her, but she wanted to be prepared. *But what did you get someone who could probably buy whatever they wanted?*

Nothing came to mind, until she walked into a store called *Christmas Time Again* at the Ridgedale Mall. She felt drawn to a snow globe portraying a singer on a stage with the words, *Christmas Time Again*, on the outside of the pedestal it rested on—the perfect gift.

She hurriedly grabbed a bite to eat at the coffee shop and headed home to change clothes.

Dressed in a Christmas red dress that snugly clung to every curve of her body as it came to just above the knee, she paired it with her black leather boots. She drove to pick up Tyler. When she arrived, his house was aglow from the multitudes of white Christmas lights.

He immediately came out and got in the car as if he'd been watching closely for her to arrive.

At the church, the parking lot looked nearly full, but she managed to find a spot in the back. They walked in and took their seats just minutes before the service started. The annual Christmas service, featured children reading segments of the Christmas story and the congregation singing the much loved and well known Christmas hymns.

It warmed her heart to hear Tyler singing loudly and with enthusiasm along with the congregation and herself. Attending church together was something she wanted for her future family and

Tyler could possibly end up being part of that. It was a good sign!

Some of the older members recognized Tyler and came over to say hello. The older people who were their parent's ages remembered him as a child. Others she felt sure knew who he was now, but they were still gracious while allowing him his privacy and welcomed him to the church.

When they arrived back at his house, he opened the garage so she could pull her car inside since it had begun snowing again. She reached into the backseat and grabbed the bag she'd brought along containing a change of clothes and Tyler's present.

"I bought a couple of steaks to grill, salad greens, baking potatoes, and an assorted tray of Christmas cookies from the bakery. And of course, wine."

While the steaks were grilling on the back patio with a low flame, they walked the short distance down to the lake. It looked frozen of course, with at least a thin coating of ice on top and covered in snow. The view was breathtaking as they could see all the houses across from them on the opposite bay, glowing from their Christmas lights. It was lightly snowing, surrounding them in an immensely romantic aura.

"It's beautiful out here," she said gazing out over the lake while sipping the hot mint cocoa in her mug.

"I'm glad you like it. Remember when we used to go to the public beach and wonder about all the people in the big houses on the lake?"

"Yes, I remember."

"Now, we're those people." He chuckled. "And if we don't want burnt steaks, we better go rescue our dinner."

***

Sitting on the couch after dinner, with only the Christmas tree lights to brighten the room, they watched the fire burning while enjoying Christmas music. It just so happened to be a CD Tyler had recorded containing his versions of the old Christmas favorites.

He'd done a great job and she would have to get a copy for

herself.

He reached over to put his arm around her shoulder and pull her closer to him. She obliged and laid her head on his shoulder.

"Did you have time to think about what we talked about yesterday?"

"Yes."

"And…" Tyler paused waiting for her answer.

"I don't want to have my heart broken again." Tara looked down afraid to meet his eyes.

"I can't make any promises except that I love you and I will give 100% to make our relationship work. I want to marry *you* and start a family." He gently tipped her chin up and kissed her, then suddenly ended the kiss.

"I have a present for you." He reached under the tree and handed her a small box.

Why was it sometimes small boxes were scary to open? What could he have gotten her? Tara slowly unwrapped it and opened the box. Shock rippled through her as she removed a ring from the box. A magnificent large—at least two carats—diamond ring. "I don't understand," she said, her voice almost a whisper.

"I know it's kind of a strange proposal, but I love you and always have. I want to marry you and make up for the last ten years of my stupidity by showing you each and every day how much I've missed you."

"But we have a lot of catching up to do, before we can have a serious talk about marriage."

"I agree, but I want you to know I am serious about getting married and us. You can hold on to it until you feel comfortable wearing it."

"And if I don't and this doesn't work out, then what?"

"You can do whatever you want with it. It's yours."

She must be crazy to even be considering his proposal, but she was thinking about it. Being together with Tyler was something she'd wanted for so long, why shouldn't she at least consider it? Slowly, she slid the ring on her finger. "I got something for you," she said and got up to get his present from her bag. She handed it to him.

He eagerly opened it and took out the snow globe. When he saw the inscription—*Christmas Time Again*—he smiled. "It will remind me of coming back to Minnesota. I love it! It's the perfect gift. Thank you." He then glanced at the ring on her finger waiting for her answer.

"I have wanted this moment to happen, forever it seems like, and now that it has, I don't see any reason to turn down your offer. Yes, I will give us a second chance."

He kissed her, a kiss that escalated both of their body temperatures. From smoldering ashes, a blazing flame rose up between them. Pausing momentarily, they both looked toward the staircase. Tyler got up and took her hand. Above the landing of the staircase, hung Christmas mistletoe. He stopped and turned her into his arms. Their lips met. Lighting a fire deep into their souls.

"Merry Christmas, Tyler," she whispered against his lips.

"Merry Christmas, Tara," he replied, his voice raspy.

She'd waited ten years to have this chance and she wasn't about to waste any more time. Tara took his hand and they walked up the dimly lit, romantic staircase. Their second chance at love would begin tonight.

From smoldering ashes came an old log's brightly burning flame.

ABOUT THE AUTHOR

Rose Marie Meuwissen, a first-generation Norwegian American born and raised in Minnesota, always tries to incorporate her Norwegian heritage into her writing. After receiving a BA in Marketing from Concordia University, a Masters in Creative Writing from Hamline University soon followed. Minnesota is still where she calls home.

She has been a member of Romance Writers of America (RWA) since 1995 and has attended multiple RWA National Conferences and Romantic Times Conventions. In 2012, she became co-founder of Romancing the Lakes of Minnesota Writers, a local RWA Chapter in Minnesota.

She has traveled around the world, including Scandinavia, but still has many places to see, enjoys attending Scandinavian events, writing conferences and is usually busy writing Contemporary and Viking Time Travel Romances, Motorcycle Rally Screenplays, Nordic Cozy Murder Mysteries, WWII Nazi Occupation of Norway Historical fiction and Norwegian Traditions Children's Books.

Visit her at:

www.rosemariemeuwissen.com

www.realnorwegianseatlutefisk.com

www.romancingtherose.blogspot.com

Taking Chances—a contemporary romance novel set in Minnesota and Arizona.

Dance of Love—a short romance story set at the Renaissance Fair in Shakopee, Minnesota, available in the anthology *Festivals of Love.*

Nor-Way to Love—a short romance story set in Minneapolis,

Minnesota on Lake Harriet, available in the anthology, *Romancing the Lakes of Minnesota—Spring.*

Blizzard of Love—a short romance story set in Lutsen, Minnesota on Lake Superior, available in the anthology, *Romancing the Lakes of Minnesota—Winter.*

Railroad Ties—a short romance story set in Two Harbors, Minnesota on Lake Superior, available in the anthology, *Romancing the Lakes of Minnesota—Autumn.*

Hot Summer Nights—a short romance story set on Prior Lake, available in the anthology, *Romancing the Lakes of Minnesota—Summer.*

Dancing in the Moonlight—a short romance story set on Mille Lacs Lake, available in the anthology, *Love in the Land of Lakes.*

Real Norwegians Eat Lutefisk—a Children's book about the tradition of Lutefisk presented in both English and Norwegian.

Real Norwegians Eat Rømmegrøt—The second Children's book in the series about the tradition of Rømmegrøt presented in both English and Norwegian.

THE ELF
Peg Pierson

Hatch Lake - Bigfork, MN

"Take this job and shov—ah. Sorry," Eirnik Krismoira said to Beldroth. Casting his gaze at the floor, once again noting how much he hated his footwear. Green velvet slippers with red bells? Seriously? Who wears slippers to work? They have zero arch support.

Beldroth scratched his beard. "Look, Eirnik, I've been your supervisor for what, two hundred years now? You're a great elf. The best electronics guy in the whole castle. You just get too worked up over things this time of year." He patted Eirnik on the shoulder. "Take the afternoon off. Go get a stiff cocoa, toss back a couple sugar cookies. Then start tomorrow fresh."

"You just don't get it," Eirnik grumbled. "I'm sick of making video games! There's more to life than *Call of Duty* and *The Legend of Zelda*."

"Ah, Eirnik. Do you know how many Elves would give their roasted chestnuts to be in your slippers? What's that new one you just designed? Where the cars and trucks play soccer?"

Eirnik, rolling his eyes, mumbled, "Rocket League. The balls explode when they score."

"See?" Beldroth slapped him on the back. "Another big hit. The kids 'll go wild for it."

"It's just a stupid game." He shot his supervisor a defiant glare. "I want my life to matter. I want to make a difference!" With that, Eirnik turned and stomped off through the high archway of the factory, through the double doors, and into the snowy arctic of the North Pole.

***

With a high-pitched shriek, the eagle dove toward Chrissy's head. The wildlife biologist ducked, letting out a scream of her own. It didn't matter how many dozens of times it happened. It always

145

scared the bejesus out of her. "Okay momma eagle, I get the hint." Chrissy took a deep breath and started climbing down the tall pine tree that hosted the bald eagle's nest.

Eggs laid in December were rare. Nesting didn't usually begin until January or February. She hated heights, but loved the eagles more. So she faced her fear again and again, to study the fierce and beautiful creatures.

After gathering up her supplies, she hopped onto her snowmobile and started for home. Her cabin on Hatch Lake was less than a mile from one of the richest eagle habitats in the state. It was her third year and she desperately hoped she could gain funding again, to keep her research going. Her mind spun back to the nest and its three eggs as she sped along the cold white path leading home, the light snowfall skimming her cheeks like frozen feathers.

Then it all stopped.

The snowmobile hit something big and hard. Chrissy went flying and landed in a deep snow bank. She heard a loud thump and then the whine of the engine puttering out.

Shaking her head, Chrissy wiped snow from her eyes and took inventory of her shaking body. Her right shoulder and hip were tender, but miraculously she seemed okay. Getting to her feet, she headed for her disabled snowmobile. She stopped in her tracks at the sight of a small man and a huge deer of some sort, both lying in the middle of the path. "Oh, my god!" Chrissy fell to her knees next to the stranger. "Are you all right?"

He moaned, sat up, and blinked his big green eyes. "Donner!" Scrambling to his feet, he took a step toward the fallen animal and shrieked. "Ah! My knee! Ouch ah—geez, this hurts."

Chrissy took his arm and helped ease him to the ground. "Here, let me help you. I'm so sorry, I didn't even see you."

The man ignored her and bent over the big deer. "Donner? Donner?" He stroked the animal's brown fur. "You okay, buddy? C'mon pal, oh please be okay!"

The animal snorted and pushed to his feet.

Chrissy tilted her head. "Why is this reindeer wearing a saddle?"

His face suddenly clouded with panic, as he replied, "Oh that." He chuckled nervously. "We were just coming back from uh—uh…"-

"Oh!" Chrissy interrupted, "You two must be part of Santa's Village. That Holiday amusement park over by Kabetogama Lake?"

His eyes brightened and his shoulders relaxed. "Yes. Yes, that's it. We're Christmas performers. Performing—Christmas stuff…Yeah, just acting like Santa's elves and reindeer. Yep, that's us."

"Again, I'm so sorry about the accident. The light is so bad at dusk here in the forest. What can I do for you? Should I call for an ambulance?"

"No!"

Chrissy startled at his reaction. "But, your knee? And you could have internal injuries."

The stranger grimaced and struggled back to his feet. "I'll be fine. No worries. Donner and I will just be on our…" The reindeer shot off into the woods like a comet. He hung his head as he finished, "…way."

***

"Thank you again, Chrissy, for your hospitality." Eirnik pulled the warm quilt up higher on his lap. Flames flickered in the fireplace casting an orange glow over the tiny living room. "Your cabin is quite cozy. But where's your Christmas tree? And holiday decorations? And manger scene?"

His hostess handed him a glass of water and a bottle of Advil. "I'm not really a Christmas person."

With a smile, he took the pills and swallowed down the glass of water, then handed everything back. She turned to walk away and the elf couldn't ignore how delightfully her derrière filled out her faded jeans. In fact, this blonde human filled out all of her clothing just perfectly. "Not a Christmas person, huh? Are you Jewish? Where's your menorah?"

147

"No, I'm not Jewish," Chrissy said returning to sit next to him on the couch. "Eir—um...I'm sorry how did you say your name?"

"Ear. Nick."

She grinned and repeated it.

The sound of his name on her tongue sent a shiver up his spine. He was beginning to feel rather elated about being hit by a snowmobile. "Seriously. Don't you like Christmas?"

Chrissy's eyes clouded. "Christmas is a time for families. I grew up going from foster home to foster home. Christmas made me feel like a third, fourth or even fifth wheel."

Now, he regretted pushing the subject. "I'm so sorry. I didn't mean to stir up bad memories and anyway, Christmas is so commercialized now. Between that and the politically correct police trying to erase its real meaning...eh, who needs it?"

She settled back on the sofa, turning toward him, allowing him a good look at her gloriously blue eyes and sensuous lips. "Enough about Christmas. You don't want medical attention. You don't want to call anyone. What am I supposed to do with you?"

Eirnik's eyebrow shot up. He squelched the images racing through his mind and cleared his throat. "Um...look, my knee feels better already. If I could just sleep on the couch here tonight, I'll leave first thing in the morning."

Chrissy pursed her mouth. "Normally, I would never allow a strange man to sleep in my cabin, but considering I ran you over, I suppose I can make an exception." She stood and started toward her bedroom. "I'll get you a blanket and pillow. Then I have to hit the hay, I need to head out early tomorrow before the next storm hits."

***

After checking her hair in the mirror, Chrissy grabbed an extra blanket and pillow from her own bed, then headed back to the strange guest. Short guys weren't normally her thing. Except Peter Dinklage...but a short guy dressed like an Elf on the Shelf? Not so much. But Eirnik had classic good looks. Bright green eyes, thick dark lashes, a strong chin, and cheekbones a supermodel would envy.

"Here you go." She set the makeshift bedding on the sofa. "I have to apologize, I'm a terrible hostess. I'm not used to having guests. Can I get you something before we turn in? I have some meatloaf in the fridge."

"Thanks. I'm not hungry, but I sure would love a cup of cocoa if you have any?"

"Hmm. I think I do." She padded into the kitchen and searched through a cupboard. "Yes! Okay, hot chocolate coming up." As she prepared the drinks she asked, "How long have you worked for Santa's Village?"

Eirnik turned and draped his arms on the back of the couch. "About three centur—um about three weeks." He quickly followed up with, "What do you do? Other than run down innocent reindeer in the woods."

"Hey!" Chrissy turned to face him, heat claiming her cheeks. "I said I was sorry. It was dusk, I didn't—"

Scrambling from the sofa, Eirnik limped as fast as he could toward Chrissy. He reached for her arm. "Hey, I'm just teasing you. It's okay, sorry, lame joke, I didn't mean to make you feel bad."

She blew out a breath then smiled. "How 'bout we call it even?"

"Deal."

They shook hands. Their eyes met and Chrissy's stomach did a little flip. "Here's your cocoa." She hastily pushed the mug into his hand and hustled back to the living room. This stranger was having a very strange effect on her hibernating libido. Living and working alone must be getting to her.

Suddenly, a loud crash came from the kitchen.

She spun around to find that Eirnik had dropped his cocoa and was wearing an expression on his face like he'd just eaten a bowl of worms.

"Eirnik! Are you all right? Was the hot chocolate too hot? Did you burn your mouth?" Chrissy's heart pounded.

"Ew, ech…ahhhh. What the hell?" He wiped at his mouth. "What was that disgusting drink?"

Chrissy pulled her brows together. "Swiss Miss. With dehydrated mini marshmallows."

"Geez. Do you maybe have some gasoline I could rinse my mouth out with?" Eirnik grumbled with a lethal stare.

Walking around the splattered mess, Chrissy picked up the mug she had made for herself and took a tiny sip. Straightening her spine, she raised her chin. "There is nothing wrong with this cocoa."

Eirnik finished wiping at his tongue with a dishtowel and threw it into the sink. "Clearly, you have never had a proper cup of cocoa." He pressed his lips into a thin line and slowly shook his head. Walking past Chrissy and the fallen mug, he proceeded to lay out his blanket and pillow for bed.

"Well, I—I've never!" Chrissy fumed.

"Never had a decent cup of hot chocolate? Is that the sentence you're searching for?" Eirnik laid down on the sofa and punched the pillow. "Maybe you can make me a nice lukewarm cup of Tasters' Choice with non-dairy creamer in the morning."

Chrissy's blood boiled. She stomped into the living room to loom over her guest. "I want you out of my house at dawn! I don't care if your knee is better or not. In fact, I hope it swells up like a bowling ball!" She whipped around and marched to her bedroom door.

Eirnik looked startled by her tirade as he sat on the couch.

Then turning back and tossing a scowl at the insolent elf impersonator cuddled on her couch, she said, "Oh, and by the way, asshole, I have a French press, freshly roasted Guatemala Antiguas coffee beans and a refrigerator stocked with *real* cream." With that, she slammed her door leaving Eirnik to himself and hopefully some nightmares.

***

The elf awoke from a restless night's sleep with a bladder as heavy as his heart. What a jerk he'd been! Living alone in his little room at the castle for three hundred years hadn't helped his social I.Q. He'd overreacted about the cocoa by biblical proportions.

He'd abandoned Santa and Beldroth to pursue a more meaningful life. To do something important. Something that mattered. So far, all he'd accomplished was losing a flying reindeer, banging up his knee, and offending a beautiful, sweet, and alluring, woman. One who'd welcomed him into her home and shown him nothing but kindness.

Plodding into the bathroom, Eirnik flicked on the light. He caught sight of his reflection in the mirror and his breath caught. He rubbed his eyes and looked again.

The buttons on his green velvet coat were gone and the seams had burst. Looking down, his pants legs ended just below his knees, and long straight toes stuck out through the tips of his slippers.

In all the excitement of the accident and the cocoa disaster, he'd completely forgotten about the conformity clause. When elves left the confines of the magical Christmas world and interacted with humans, their bodies transformed to blend in with the local inhabitants.

Eirnik shed the shredded remains of his elf suit and put on a pink robe that hung inside the bathroom door.

So much for leaving at dawn. Donner had taken off with all his money, his street clothes for post-conformity, and his cell phone. With slumped shoulders, the elf excited the powder room and hoped that Chrissy had an extraordinarily bad short-term memory.

***

The scent of fresh brewed coffee kick started the wildlife biologist's brain waves. Chrissy pulled a thick cardigan around her and followed her nose out to the kitchen.

Her sleep dusted eyes widened. There in her kitchen stood a tall, handsome man wearing her bathrobe and scrambling eggs.

"Oh, good morning," he said, turning from the stove to face her. "I know you wanted me out first thing, but I hoped maybe I could change your mind with some eggs Eirnik style and your wonderful coffee. It really is fantastic. I'm so sorry about the whole cocoa debacle. I was a dick. I'm just not used to being around people very often."

Chrissy blinked, rubbed her eyes and tilted her head to the side. "Eirnik?" Short and in the elf suit he'd been good looking. Tall, and in her bathrobe he was drop dead gorgeous. Broad shoulders and serious biceps showed under the thin pink fabric. He turned back to the stove and his tight bottom practically made her swoon. She licked her dry lips.

"You're…big." Was all she could manage.

He gave a low sexy growl. "Well, I'm not one to brag, but actually—"

"No!" She covered her face with her hands. "That's not what I meant!" She took a hesitant step forward and wiggled her fingers at him. "You're tall. And big. Last night you were what? Like well under five feet? You probably couldn't have ridden a roller coaster at Valley Fair."

Which is exactly what Chrissy's body felt like. A roller coaster riding tracks of fear, disbelief, curiosity, anger, and a long home stretch of lust.

Eirnik plated up the eggs, poured her a cup of coffee and tightened the belt of the robe. While cooking it had loosened, leaving a long span of masculine chest available for ogling. "What do you like in your coffee?"

"Cream please." Chrissy stumbled into a chair at her little kitchen table. "I'm very, very confused. How could you grow this much overnight? You're like Tom Hanks in Big."

Eirnik sat down and sipped his coffee. "Chrissy, I'm just going to tell you the truth. I'm a real Christmas elf. I got fed up with making toys and left the North Pole to pursue a more vital, meaningful life." He took another long draw from his drink. "When elves enter the Human Realm our bodies acclimate to our surroundings. It's called a conformity clause. That's why I grew from elf size to man size overnight." He stood up and retrieved the French press, pouring them both more of the delicious brew. "Now, I need your help again. When Donner ran off, he took all my stuff with him.

I have no clothes or money."

The roller coaster emotion ride sped into overdrive. Chrissy started to panic. She wondered if the glass coffee maker could knock out the crazy lunatic sitting in her bathrobe. Then she looked into his clear green eyes. A sweep of empathy washed through her veins. She didn't believe a word he said, of course, but *he* certainly did. Somehow, she knew he wasn't a danger. He really did need her help. "Alright. Eirnik. I'll help you."

Eirnik grinned and dropped to his knees wrapping his big hands around hers. The robe flashed open again, this time distracting Chrissy with a muscled thigh worthy of a Magic Mike movie.

"Thank you! Oh, thank you! I really appreciate it. It's great you believe me. I'm impressed. Not everyone would have such an open mind about this."

"Whoa now." Chrissy stood up forcing him to drop her hands and stand as well. He towered over her and his shoulders seem to span the entire kitchen. Her girly parts sprung to life, but crazy is crazy. "I didn't say I believed you. I said I'd help you. I have some work I have to get done right now, but when I get back, I'll take you somewhere to get the kind of help you need."

Tilting his head, Eirnik smacked his lips. "You think I'm nuts. You're gonna call someone and have me carted off to a looney bin." He straightened. "Thanks, but I'll pass." Then moving swiftly, he snatched his too small elf hat from the couch and stretched it over his head. He put his hand on the doorknob to leave. "Thank you for your hospitality. I'll just be off now for some frostbite and animal mauling. Have a nice life." Opening the door an icy wind blew through the cabin lifting his flimsy housecoat up revealing the most gorgeous ass Chrissy had ever seen.

If lust and guilt had a baby, it would be the emotion the wildlife biologist felt. The man had to be out of his mind but she couldn't let him leave in the twenty-degree weather. "Wait." She trotted over. "You're right. I do think you're crazy, but maybe you just have some temporary sanity amnesia."

His brows drew together. "Is that even a thing?"

Chrissy sighed. "No. I don't think so. But let's just go with it till I figure out something better."

***

The Eagle soared above them. Eirnik watched Chrissy as she shot pictures of the regal bird with her elaborate camera equipment. He whispered, "Why did you become a biologist? Have you always liked birds?"

She captured a few more shots, lowered the camera and whispered back, "Not liked. Loved." She caught his gaze with her blue eyes.

Heat rushed Eirnik's body at her last word. He wasn't crazy, but the feelings springing to life in his heart were. They barely knew each other. Who was he kidding? Chrissy was an educated no-nonsense human with a masters in wildlife biology. She studied and rescued bald eagles. Her life meant something. She meant something. All he'd ever mastered was making video games.

He didn't matter to anyone.

"Hey, earth to Eirnik?" Chrissy's said, tapping him on the shoulder of his new parka. Before heading out to her study site in the woods, she'd stopped at a clothing store and outfitted him in snow pants, a flannel shirt, and a trapper hat. "Listen, I need to climb up and check on the nest. You just stay here and be quiet. Okay?"

He nodded and smiled.

The lines on her beautiful face tensed as she started up the tree.

When she finally reached the branch near the nest, the elf sighed in relief.

Chrissy looked down, giving him a thumbs up and a halfhearted smile.

He suddenly wished they could trade places.

In the clear blue sky, Eirnik noticed the big momma eagle soaring back. He stood up sending the powdery snow to swish around his new boots, wondering if he should try and warn Chrissy of her return to her eggs, or what might be babies now.

A loud thundering crack sliced the frigid morning air. Eirnik jumped, letting out a shout, followed by the echoes of Chrissy's shriek.

Looking skyward, Eirnik shouted, "Chrissy, are you...?" His words died in his throat.

Momma Eagle was dropping from the sky. Fast.

The Christmas elf watched in horror, knowing the pain that would be searing through Chrissy's heart.

Suddenly, the bird flapped her great wings and slowed her descent.

Chrissy scrambled from the tree and the pair dashed as fast as the snow would allow to where she had fallen.

Chrissy's eyes glistened with tears. She gently picked up momma eagle and examined the damage inflicted by a gunshot. Raising her head, she looked at Eirnik with a fierce fury. "Poachers. Those mother fucking bastards!"

"Will she live? Can we get her to an animal doctor?" Eirnik asked feeling useless.

Chrissy softly petted the birds white head. "She's bleeding badly. It'll take over an hour to get to a vet. We'd need a miracle for her to survive."

A miracle.

The simple words blasted Eirnik like a nuclear light bulb had illuminated over his head. He picked up a handful of snow and started singing. Singing in a language, few humans ever heard. It was pure and glorious, like the dawn of a new day.

She sniffled. "What are you doing?"

He finished the song and grinned. "Giving you a Christmas miracle." The elf delicately blew a thin coating of the enchanted snow over the wound on the momma eagle.

Moments later, the eagle jerked and rolled up onto her talons. She stood in the snow, blinked, and stepped toward Eirnik. She lowered her head in a gesture of thanks.

The elf gently caressed the beautiful avian creature on her regal head. He shifted his gaze to Chrissy and said, "Merry Christmas."

***

Chrissy's hands were still shaking when they returned to the cabin. After notifying the local authorities, she tried to track the criminals herself. But after two hours, Eirnik finally convinced her they were long gone, and that allowing a miracle to cause an elf to freeze to death in the icy tundra of Minnesota was not the ideal way to spend Christmas Eve.

The fireplace was roaring. Chrissy huddled on the little sofa watching the flames, wondering if they gave couples discounts at mental health facilities.

The front door banged open sending in a whirl of snowflakes, a very handsome rather tall elf, and a fragrant Fraser fir about three foot tall. He stood the small tree up on the floor by the window. Brushing himself off, Eirnik slanted a look at Chrissy. "I know you're not into Christmas, but can I please just have it for tonight? I'll decorate it and take it down myself. You don't have to lift a finger."

His expectant and utterly irresistible expression sent waves of emotion zinging through every fiber of Chrissy's being.

It was crazy.

He was crazy.

She was crazy!

She couldn't deny it. She was crazy about Eirnik, the elf. She may have crashed into his reindeer, but he'd crashed into her life with a bang, igniting desires and feelings she'd never had in her life. And he saved the life of momma eagle.

"Well?" Eirnik asked. "Can I keep it?"

Chrissy popped up from the cushions. "Of course, you can keep your Christmas tree Eirnik." She stepped closer and pinned his green eyes with a stare. "If you want, we can drive in to town before all the stores close and get decorations. And gourmet cocoa. Anything you want. I don't know how you did it but thank you again for helping the eagle. You're my Christmas hero."

He clasped her hands and pulled her close. His chest only inches away from her face. "I'm no hero. I'm just happy I had enough magic left in me to save her."

Chrissy wanted nothing more than to run her fingers in his hair and bring her lips to his.

So she did.

***

Eirnik gasped as Chrissy's lips claimed his own. He quickly regained his composure, deepening the kiss, wrapping his hands around her waist and pulling her body in tight to his own.

Nothing had ever felt this right or this natural. He wanted to kiss, touch and caress every inch of her. She tasted of coffee and smelled like fresh wilderness. Her hands mimicked his, exploring his shoulders, arms and chest. Their breathing erratic, hot, sensual as passion hung in the air between them.

"Uh, Eirnik?" Panting, Chrissy let loose of the elf. "I'm sorry. I shouldn't have kissed you. We barely know each other."

"Yeah, you're right." Eirnik nodded, letting go of her for one second, and then planted another searing kiss on her ripe lips. She felt so soft and desirable. His mouth slowly moved down her neck, nibbling and teasing.

Chrissy squirmed and leaned in closer, arching her neck to allow him better access. She groaned, "We—should—um—really…"

Eirnik stopped sucking her earlobe and gazed into her in her crystal blue eyes. "Chrissy, I know it's crazy, but I've never felt this way before. Ever. And I'm over three centuries old, so that's really saying something."

Chrissy's eyes widened and she grinned like a Cheshire cat. "That's it!" She grabbed his hand in hers and yanked him toward the bedroom. "We're crazy! We are in no way responsible for our actions."

Together, they tumbled onto her bed. Winter sunlight filtered through the blinds bathing them in a golden glow as they explored and worshipped each other. Both reached that pinnacle of ecstasy, quickly, and easily as if their bodies had been entwined for eternity.

After a while, and now, laying with Chrissy in his arms, the Christmas elf felt happiness like he had never imagined.

It couldn't last. He didn't deserve her. Her work was vital. His work was silly. Even if she were happy with him right now, which, if judging by her screams of delight a few minutes ago, seemed pretty obvious…it wouldn't last.

Chrissy was a wildlife biologist. He was a Christmas elf. Eirnik sighed and kissed her perfect blonde head. If he believed for a second this could last, then maybe he really was crazy.

***

A heavy knock on the front door roused Chrissy from her sublime slumber. She rubbed her eyes and slid out from under Eirnik's embrace. Pulling on the pink bathrobe he'd been wearing earlier, she found herself sniffing at the fabric, inhaling his scent. God, the man made her crazy. Literally, it seemed.

Barefoot, she padded across the cold hardwood floor to the door. "I'm coming." Who could be at her doorstep on Christmas Eve? She didn't have any family, and her closest friend was sitting on a nest of eggs at the moment.

She opened the door.

A short man with pointed ears, a green velvet suit, and a scowl, said, "Hello. Is Eirnik here?" The huge reindeer behind him snuffled, sending white mist from his nostrils.

Chrissy hesitated. Her heart raced. The craziness swept through her again. Her legs began to give out but strong arms came to the rescue, scooping her up.

"Beldroth?" Eirnik asked as he held Chrissy in his arms. "What are you doing here? How did you find me?"

Beldroth hooked his thumb toward the Reindeer. "Donner told me. So…uh, how 'bout you go put on some clothes and we'll get going."

Sobering up, Chrissy realized that Eirnik was stark naked. She wrangled out of his hold and placed her body in front of him. "He's not going anywhere, Mr. Beldroth."

"It's just Beldroth, sweetie. And he IS coming with me." The elf shivered. "Could we move this inside, I'm freezing my jingle bells off out here." Without further ado, he pushed past Chrissy and scurried over to the fire stretching out his palms.

Donner turned to nibble on a potted plant. Eirnik said hello to the reindeer and then closed the front door on his furry friend.

"Honey, why don't you go put your pants on," Chrissy suggested when her honey joined her and Beldroth at the fire.

Eirnik snickered and headed back to the bedroom.

She rounded on the new elf in her cabin. "Look, I'm sorry to be rude, but Eirnik left the North Pole because he was unhappy. I think you should respect his decision."

Beldroth rubbed his short beard. "I wish I could—uh...?"

"Chrissy," she supplied.

"Okay, Chrissy, I wish I could." He gave her the once over. A grin pulled at the corner of his mouth. "Clearly, he is enjoying himself out here in the human world. But Mr. C is having a conniption fit. It's Christmas Eve for heaven's sake! Nobody can make video games like Eirnik." The elf cast his gaze to the floor, then popped his head up and seared her with a bold stare. "Thousands of children won't receive their Christmas wishes. You probably don't believe me, but Santa is real. The truth is that we make the toys that kids want. Eirnik designs and produces hundreds of video games. Fun, zany, educational, you name it. Eirnik can make it. He's an innovator."

Chrissy glanced over at the little Christmas tree sitting proud, covered in paper snowflakes and a tinfoil star that Eirnik had lovingly made. "Christmas is important to him. He cherishes it. But he needs something more in his life. He wants his life to matter."

Sticking his hands to his hips, Beldroth said, "Eirnik does matter! Nobody at the castle can do what he does. The children need him. Please, Chrissy. Let him come home and do what he was born to do. What matters more than a child's smile on Christmas morning?"

***

Eirnik listened from behind the bedroom door.

He wasn't important. Gaming was not important.

Eirnik made his way into the living room and wrapped an arm around Chrissy's waist. "Beldroth, thank you, but I'm staying here. Chrissy is a wildlife biologist. She does ground breaking studies of bald eagles. A whole species benefits from her work." He turned to Chrissy. "You do want me to stay? Don't you? I can help you in the field. You have to admit, you could use an assistant."

Watching her face, the elf's heart sank.

"Eirnik," Chrissy said not meeting his eyes. "You're a great guy—elf, and I'm sure you'd make a wonderful assistant, but your friend here is right. The children of the world need you more than I do. I know what it's like to wake up and find nothing under the tree." She then hurried into the kitchen and furiously began cleaning.

Eirnik swallowed hard. He ached for her to rush back to his arms and beg him to stay. Beg him to stay in her life, in her heart, and oh, please…in her bed.

That didn't happen.

"Thanks for everything, Chrissy," he said putting on his new shoes and coat. "C'mon Beldroth. Lets' go."

The front door made a loud click as the Christmas elves left with the reindeer clomping after them.

Eirnik couldn't see it, but the wildlife biologist's tears were rolling down her face and into the kitchen sink.

***

Three Months Later…

The young eaglets chirped and soared, flapping their freshly unfurled wings into the afternoon sky. Chrissy snapped off a slew of photo's, smiling—a rarity these long cold days. She clipped the lens cover on and turned to gather the rest of her equipment. Her breath caught in her throat. There in the woods stood a man.

Her heart sped.

Eirnik stood tall, hands on hips and legs wide. "Chrissy," he said sternly, "I've made my entire quota of video games for this year. I'll have to go back to the Pole right after thanksgiving, but that's eight months away." He started toward her, the hard snow crunching under his boots. "You may still think I'm crazy, but I'm in love with you."

He stopped so close, she could feel his breath on her lips.

He cupped her cheek with his hand. "Please tell me you want me to stay."

She couldn't resist. Chrissy stood on her tiptoes, grabbed Eirnik, tangled her hands in his hair and crushed her mouth to his. He kissed her back with all the love and desire she'd been dreaming about for months.

They ended the kiss after a couple of minutes.

"Eirnik, I'm an idiot. I should never have let you go. I was miserable without you." She nibbled on his lip because she just had to, then continued, "But what about changing your life? You were so unhappy being a Christmas elf."

With a grin he said, "You and Beldroth helped me understand. The games may seem trivial, but the way they make kids feel on the most special of day of the year is not." He ducked in for another searing kiss that made Chrissy want to jump his bones right there in the snow.

Mama eagle flew overhead. Eirnik abruptly halted what had become a full blown make-out session. "Chrissy! I forgot! This is the best part. Mr. C wants you to come with me when I return. He wants you to help us with a whole new line of toys about eagles. And other birds and animals too. He wants to teach kids about nature, and helping to preserve the environment, so that all species can live in harmony."

Chrissy hesitated. She'd lived alone for so long. "I don't know Eirnik. It's a wonderful idea. I can continue my research here, then go with you part of the year. But...all those elves? How do you know they'll accept me?"

"They'll accept you because I love you. You'll be working side by side with all of us Christmas elves. We're a family up there, Chrissy. You'll be part of it."

"You know, you were the one who wanted to change his life. Not me."

"Just tell me you'll come."

She bit her lip, then smiled. "Okay. You've convinced me."

Eirnik shivered. "Let's go back to the cabin," he said wiggling his brows. "We only have eight months till we leave for the Pole."

Chrissy smiled and took his hand. "I love you, you sexy elf, you."

He kissed her forehead with a loud smack. "I love you too. Just promise me one thing."

"Anything."

"You'll leave the cocoa making to me."

The End

ABOUT THE AUTHOR

Peg Pierson writes paranormal comedy romance. Her debut novel, *Flirting with Fangs,* is available on Amazon, with its sequel, *Flirting with Fairies,* coming soon! She resides in the Twin Cities area where you can find her every fall haunting the register at Halloween Express!

peg@flirtingwithfangs.com
http://pegpierson.squarespace.com

THE LAST CUSTOMER ON CHRISTMAS EVE
Ann Nardone

Lake Winnibigoshish - Bena, MN

Aurora Boulais Cabin Resort Bar & Grille

"Good night and merry Christmas." Lisa Calloway waved as most of the evening's customers went out the door. On a normal night, the bar and grille at the Aurora Boulais Cabin Resort would be open for a few more hours. Tonight was not a normal night. Tomorrow morning, this room would be filled with aunts, uncles and cousins keeping up the family tradition going back to her great grandparents' time. Only one cabin was occupied by someone other than her relatives and the desk clerk must have warned them that on Christmas, the restaurant was closed.

She listened to the snowmobiles pulling away to beat the coming of night. The locals were heading home across the wide expanse of Lake Winnibigoshish. Only one customer remained, a man at the farthest table from the bar. His back was to her and he seemed to be staring out the window into the darkness.

Humming, "Hark the Herald Angels Sing" to herself, Lisa gathered up the remaining beer mugs. If she saved the dishes for later, she would be able to wash the tables and close out the register then still have time to get ready to meet her parents for church at ten.

She'd already sent the bartender home, but she didn't mind closing up alone. She did however, wonder what to do about the night's last guest, who showed no signs of leaving. With any luck, he would notice her shutting down and take the hint. If not, she would have to flat out tell him it was time to go. Then she felt a stab of sympathy. It was Christmas Eve, why was he sitting here alone?

"You've always had a wonderful voice, Lisa," the man said in the smooth Louisiana drawl she'd never forgotten. He stood up and turned to face her. "It's good to see you again."

She halted and her mouth fell open. She had to take in a gulp of air before she could speak, "Matthew De Le Crouix." This couldn't be real. He couldn't just show up here after all this time and expect her to even be glad to see him. Or to be nice to him. "We're closed."

"I know. " He folded his arms across his broad chest. "I wanted to talk to you alone."

"We have nothing to talk about anymore."

His eyes—those gorgeous green eyes, met hers. "You look as beautiful as you sound."

He didn't mean it, she was sure. She'd dressed in an oversized red and green sweater with yoga pants, her hair back in a messy ponytail. But what did it matter? She didn't need to impress him. "And you're wearing flannel. Trying to fit in, in Northern Minnesota?"

"Just trying to stay warm."

"Oh, this is nothing." With undue force, she began wiping off the table next to him. "It must be twenty, twenty-five degrees out there. Warm for this time of year. It won't last though. It will be below zero by New Year's. But I'm sure you'll be back in the Big Easy by then. You never did stick around long." She moved to the next table, her feet stomping across the hardwood floor.

"I'm not sure how long I'll be here. But I haven't lived in New Orleans for a long time." He moved closer to her. "Aren't you even going to ask?"

"Ask what, Matthew?" She hoped she sounded indifferent. "Ask why you're here? Or where you've been the last ten years."

"Eleven."

"Whatever." Lisa dropped the towel. It landed with a thump on the pine table top. "I used to care. I waited for you. I tried calling. I tried writing. I searched the internet for anything on you. Then I got over it. I moved on."

"Are you married now?" He actually sounded worried.

"No," she replied and instantly regretted not lying. "Not because I've been pining for you. I've had boyfriends. But mostly, I've been doing other things. I've taken over managing the resort. And I still write songs. Some good ones actually. A couple of bands have recorded some of my stuff."

A smile crossed his lips. A real one *maybe*. "I know. I've followed you on line. You've always been talented but you just keep getting better."

"Thank you," she said after a long pause. She picked the towel up off the table and walked back behind the bar, hoping he would feel awkward standing there.

"I still play guitar," Matthew called after her. "I'm not trying to be a rock star anymore, but I still play. I play the songs you wrote for me."

Now it made sense. She almost laughed. "Is that what this is about? You want the rights to those songs? Coming all the way up here is extreme, even for you. You could have sent an email."

"What?" He looked genuinely surprised. "You can't honestly think…Oh, man, I've really messed this up."

She typed the password into the register, her head down. She knew she would not be able to concentrate on counting the money but she could fake it. That way, he would not be able to see her face. She didn't want him to see the color in her cheeks.

Matthew reached across the bar and touched her hand.

She jerked it away.

"Lisa, I'm sorry. Please listen to me. This has nothing to do with song rights or anything like that. I came to explain. And to tell you I love you. I've loved you all this time."

Once this would have been a Christmas wish come true. But not anymore. Now, she just wanted him out of her bar, so she could salvage a little of her holiday spirit. "I don't have time for any of this," she said, slamming the drawer shut without running the totals. "I'm meeting my family at church, because you know…it's Christmas Eve."

He stood there in front of her, not moving. He was as handsome as he'd ever been but something in his eyes had changed. He wasn't the boy she'd known. He was a man who'd seen sorrow.

"I don't want to hear it. It doesn't matter anymore." She intended to walk away, to leave him standing alone in the middle of the dark, empty bar. Instead, she stood, staring back at him.

Matthew finally spoke, "That night we met, in Minneapolis. I was playing at First Avenue. There I was, on that stage where so many greats had played. I didn't think it could get any better than that. Then I looked out and saw you. And you know, that's what I've always remembered about it. Not playing my dream gig, but meeting you."

She wasn't going to tell him how many times she thought about that night herself. "I was a dumb college kid then. I've changed."

"But some things don't change, do they? Not really."

"Did you come all this way to discuss philosophy?" Lisa knew she was being harsh. And she knew he deserved it.

"No." He took a deep breath. "I want to introduce you to someone. My son."

"Your—son? You have a son?" So he hadn't been pining for her all these years either. "Where is he?"

"He's just back at the cabins. Come on. I want y'all to meet."

Whatever Matthew had been to her eleven years ago, he was indeed a different man now. A cold and selfish one. "You left a child alone in a strange place. What kind of a father are you?"

"Oh no, it's all right," he said quickly. "He's old enough. He's thirteen."

The number hung in the air between them. Any flicker of forgiveness she'd started to feel—froze. This night couldn't get any worse. "Oh, I see," she said, her voice rising with each syllable. "So everything was a lie. You didn't just walk out on me. You walked out on someone else first. Oh, my God! Were you married then? Was I your—?"

He raised his hands as if to ward off a blow. "No, no. Nothing like that. His mother and I were never good together. We'd split before I ever met you, before I ever did that tour."

"So he was just a little detail that slipped your mind?"

Matthew paced in front of her. "I don't think I could have done this any worse. I should have told you. I was going to. I knew I had to tell you before I proposed. But your family is so important to you. I didn't know what you'd think if you found out I had left my own child for my ex-wife to raise alone."

"Well, you're right. I wouldn't have been impressed. But I would have definitely preferred the truth. As compared to you, keeping that from me."

"I know that now. But I was young. I'd already screwed up one relationship. And I was afraid of losing you." He reached out for her hand again, but withdrew it. In the dim light of the bar, he looked lost. "I'd like you to meet him. He wants to meet you. He's heard so much about you."

This was pointless, but it also seemed pointless to refuse. "Fine. And then I really do have to go."

Matthew gave her small smile and went back to his table to get his coat.

Her jacket sat tucked under the bar and as she slipped into it, she was already starting to regret agreeing.

They walked the short distance to the Aurora Boulais cabins in silence. The sky was clear with the temperature dropping, but the moonlight lit the way.

"Beau, I have someone here to meet you," Matthew said, as he unlocked the door and they stepped into the warmth of the log-lined front room.

A lanky boy looking like a thirteen-year-old version of Matthew was laying on the couch, a game controller in his hands. As he looked up at them, his face broke into a wide grin.

"Lisa, this is my boy, Beau."

The pride in his voice reduced her anger just a little.

The boy jumped to his feet and stood as straight as someone his age could manage. "I'm pleased to meet you," he greeted shyly and held out a skinny hand.

Lisa smiled and shook it. "Hi, Beau. It's nice to meet you, too." She looked around the cabin. It seemed cozy, with a fire crackling in the fireplace and the smell of ginger cookies coming from the kitchenette, but there was no tree or decorations, only a few presents piled on the birch wood coffee table. Not the way for a kid to spend Christmas. "I just came to invite you and your dad to dinner with me and my family tomorrow. I have a couple of cousins about your age. They like video games, too." She didn't even know where this unexpected invite came from. She gripped her hands together to steady herself.

Matthew hid his surprise at her sudden offer fairly well. "Would you like that, buddy?"

"Yeah!" Beau's grin grew wider. "I mean, that would be great. Thank you."

"Well, good. I will see you both at the grille at one tomorrow." She turned to Matthew and all the warmth disappeared from her demeanor. "If that works for you?"

"It will be my pleasure." He seemed more cheerful now.

However, for Lisa nothing had changed. She turned to leave.

"I'm going to walk Miss Lisa home," he said.

She didn't protest when he followed her out the door.

The air felt cold but there was no wind. The moonlight sparkled on the snow like diamonds. They stopped under a tall pine.

Lisa took a moment to choose her words. "Beau seems like a great kid."

"He is."

"I didn't want him to miss out on all that is Christmas. But then I want you to leave. Having you here is just too difficult for me."

"Because you still love me?"

She didn't even have the energy to get angry. "I did once. Now I'm just hurt."

Matthew looked past her, out toward Lake Winnie. "Do you remember that time you brought me up here. Had me meet your parents and see the resort?"

Yes, she remembered it well. She'd thought then they were going to get married. She'd thought he loved her. That they had a whole future together. "I do."

"We were standing out on the dock. It was this perfect day, warm and sunny. Everything was blue and green and it all smelled so fresh. And I asked what it was you liked about the winters here. You said it's just as beautiful but in a different way. I had a hard time believing it then, but you were right."

"Do you think a few memories are going to get me to change my mind?" She turned to look him square in the eye. "I can't," she spoke calmly, fighting to keep her anger at bay. "I loved you so much. You were my world. And then you told me you were going down south to take care of some business. You promised you would come back, but you didn't. Not until now. And I find out you were hiding a child and an ex-wife you never told me about? I find out you yanked your son away at Christmas to chase after me. I don't know why you left. I don't know why you suddenly showed up again."

"Can we talk about this inside?" he asked with a noticeable shiver.

"No."

He chuckled. "Alright." He took her hand.

This time, she didn't pull it back. She could share that much warmth with him.

"I was a little wild when I was young. Maybe it was the whole rock and roller thing. I don't know. But I don't think you would have liked me much then. Evie was the same way. We didn't fall in love, exactly. We just kind of got together. We didn't plan on a baby. We should have tried harder to be good parents and to make our relationship work. We just weren't strong enough people, maybe. So when she told me to leave, I went without a fight."

"What about Beau?"

"She wanted sole custody, so I let her have it. I know how wrong it was, but I kind of saw it as an escape. I joined the band, went on tour. I missed him, but I convinced myself he was better off without me. Then we got the gig at First Ave and I met you." He looked down and kicked at the snow. "We were nothing like it'd been with Evie. I wanted to settle down with you. I figured we would get married. I'd get Beau summers and we'd have kids together. Be a family."

Lisa felt a tear hot against the cool skin of her cheek. "Why didn't that happen?"

"Evie called me out of blue. She said she couldn't handle things anymore. I didn't know how to explain it to you, so I left. I wasn't lying when I said I'd be back. I thought I'd be able to go down home and set up a visitation schedule. It didn't work out that way." Matthew looked saddened.

"Did you—did you get back together with her?" She took in a breath with the question.

He shook his head and gave a small, ugly laugh. "Nothing like that. Evie was…troubled. She needed to get away. So she left. She calls Beau once or twice a year, but we've only seen her a dozen times since then."

"That poor boy!"

"So you see, I had my hands full. I got a job that had us moving a lot. Beau needed all my attention. And I couldn't ask you to take all that on. Not after I had kept so much from you already."

"You could have let me make that choice."

He nodded slowly. "I told you, I made a lot of mistakes."

Lisa leaned against the rough bark of the tree. "Alright, I understand. I'm not saying I think you were right, but I get it." She let go of his hand. "But why show up now? On Christmas, no less."

"It was Beau's idea."

Even in the darkness, she could see pride light his face.

"About a week ago. We were eating dinner, not saying much because he's at this age where he doesn't say a whole lot to me. Then out of the blue, he asked why I didn't have a wife or a girlfriend. So I told him the truth. I had fallen in love with an amazing girl, and then blew it. He said I should give it another try. At first, I thought he was just being a kid, expecting a happy ending to come easy. But I wanted to think like a kid again, too. Next thing I knew, we were loading up the car and heading here."

With this heartfelt speech, she knew he was telling the truth. The sweet idea of making something impossible happen, coming from a kid, just hit her in the chest. Tears formed in her eyes at the part where Matthew said she was the girl he'd loved and lost. She looked around at the white of the snow and the fog from their breaths. She had been a little harsh in telling him to leave when he came to the bar tonight. She looked up at him and wiped her eyes. "I'm not kicking you out. You can stay as long as you want."

"Good thing you feel that way because we're not going anywhere. I mean we'll leave the resort as soon as I find a house. I'll get some kind of job. I hear the schools are really good here, so I think Beau will like it."

She shook her head. "That's not what I meant. Matthew, we can't get back together. Not after everything."

He grinned, just like Beau had. "You say that now. Give me the chance. I bet after a few months, we'll be talking marriage again."

"You won't last a few months. You won't be able to take the cold."

"Oh, yeah?" He unzipped his jacket and slipped it off, letting it fall to the ground. "For you, I can handle anything."

She laughed in spite of herself. "You're crazy and you will freeze to death if you're not careful."

"Just showing you how much cold I can put up with if I have to."

Her phone buzzed in her pocket. She fished it out and stared at the ID. "It's my mom," she said without answering it. "I really have to go. But I'll see you tomorrow."

"And after tomorrow?" he asked with hope in his voice.

Lisa tried not to look into those mesmerizing eyes, or feel the heat she'd always felt from just hearing his voice. "I don't know. Maybe. We'll have to see if you don't die of hypothermia before then."

"I won't. I think there's a thaw coming." His eyes twinkled at her.

***

The day had been wonderful. Her family had welcomed Beau with open arms. They treated Matthew nice enough, but they did seem a little leery since they knew she'd had her heart broken by him years ago.

Beau seemed to soak up the camaraderie he'd been offered by her cousins, as most were close to his age as well. The boys talked about school and music, video games and the latest horror films, of all things.

Matthew had remained at her side through most of the festivities and when it all ended, he gave her a light kiss on the cheek, then took Beau back to the cabin.

That evening, when she got home, she really thought about what all he'd said the night before. Did he really believe he could work a miracle here? Matthew still seemed determined to have a life here and he'd even had a job offer from one of her uncles.

Every night when she closed the bar, Matthew showed up and walked her home. Even after he'd gotten the job at the hotel and was working.

Lisa did feel herself thawing toward him, but she kept hiding her true feelings. Too afraid he would just up and leave one day.

Then after a month, she knew she was in trouble, they were meeting for lunches. Having dinner together at her parents every Sunday after church. He'd shown up at her church for service, three weeks back. He and Beau attended every Sunday after that.

Could this really work out? A new chance for them, all because of a young boy who encouraged his father to make it happen?

Now today, Matthew called and asked her out to dinner. Then, she actually said yes! Lisa knew she should have refused, but she herself was beginning to see them together. She just needed some sign, something to tell her, he meant everything he said.

***

They sat in the restaurant, having dessert after they enjoyed a great dinner. They laughed and talked about Beau, her parents and his new job.

Matthew kept touching her hand and looking into her eyes.

It became harder and harder to resist the man she'd loved for all these years. He'd been right…she did still love him.

"So, I wanted to tell you something." He reached across the table and took her hand.

Lisa sucked in a breath. What did he want? Could she even give it? Or was it some news she wouldn't want to hear?

He smiled and patted her hand. "It isn't huge. It's just…" His voice fell away.

"Did your ex come back?" she blurted out. "Oh, I know…She wants you back!"

His eyes widened. "No."

"Oh, so you are moving back south then?"

He shook his head and laughed. "Again…no."

She sighed. "Then what?"

Matthew grabbed both of her hands. "I am staying. I even plan to beef up my collection of parkas, gloves, snow boots and long johns. So, no…there will be no leaving and no one else is coming." He grinned at her.

Lisa let out the breath she didn't even know she'd been holding. "Then what is it?"

He reached into his pocket.

Lisa watched him closely as he raised a little velvet ring box. "OH!" She swallowed heavily and shook her head.

He held his other hand up to stop her from saying anything else. "No…no." He chuckled. "I simply want to show you something, for now."

Lisa trembled. What was this all about? He wasn't asking her the *big* question, yet he had a ring box?

Matthew opened the box and pulled out a receipt. It looked

yellowed and scrunched. "Take the slip, please?"

With a shaky hand, Lisa did just that. She smoothed it out and stared at the print on it. "Eleven hundred and fifty dollars," she read out loud.

Matthew laughed. "Yeah, that is in bad taste for you to see the actual price, but I can say if it had been bought today, it would have sold for at least double that."

Lisa felt confused. "What do you mean, today?"

"Read the whole receipt Lisa," he urged.

Her startled gaze dropped to the slip again. Her eyes widened. "You bought this..." Her words faded as shock took hold.

Matthew nodded. "Eleven years ago."

Her eyes shot up and met his. "You mean you were going to—?"

"Yeah." He looked saddened for the first time in all these weeks. "I was going to ask you to marry me."

Lisa felt tears fill her eyes.

"I kept this ring all this time."

"Why, Matt? Why?"

He grabbed the ring out of the box. "I couldn't let that dream go, I guess. Even when I knew it wasn't possible for it to ever come true. I think I looked at this ring so many times over the years, I'm surprised it isn't worn down and falling apart." He raised his gaze to hers. "I found out that even in the south, you can freeze almost to death. The cold of being without you, kept me frozen inside. I'd thought you probably were married and had moved on and well...I used all the excuses to avoid coming here and facing you after all that I'd done. But you know what? I am here and I will stay here. Till your ice thaws. Cause without you, I will forever be cold and empty."

Lisa's throat swelled up and she couldn't swallow.

"You don't have to say anything. You don't have to accept it. But the ring is yours, always has been."

Tears rolled down her cheeks as she took the ring from him.

He bit at his lip as she studied the beautiful piece of jewelry.

Gold inlay, a nearly three-carat diamond with tiny diamond clusters on each side. A ring that was perfect for her. She slipped it on her finger.

His eyes widened, as he now seemed unable to speak.

"I think you'd better forget about parkas and snow boots."

Matthew gulped heavily and stared at her face.

"Because it is almost spring, ya know?" Lisa smiled through her tears.

With tears in his eyes, Matthew lifted her hand and kissed it.

ABOUT THE AUTHOR

Ann Nardone's stories appear in Romancing the Lakes Summer, Fall, Winter and Spring anthologies. She balances writing with working at her job, raising her teenagers, caring for a menagerie of pets and spending time with her husband and his beloved '66 Impala. She lives in Farmington.

ABOUT THE MINNESOTA LAKES WRITERS

Living in Minnesota, surrounded by lakes, *Minnesota Lakes Writers* can't help creating stories of being up North at the cabin, in town at one of the city lakes or Minnesota's own massive Lake Superior. No matter what time of year it is, there is always something going on at the lake. Hey, it's Minnesota! Whether you are sitting on a dock listening to loons calling, taking a leisurely walk around a lake, cruising the lake on a boat or just sitting on a beach, for writers, ideas form and stories begin.

These writers enjoy getting together to set in motion scary stories to be told under the evening stars at a beach campfire or on the frozen ice of Minnesota's winter lakes. And, of course, romances set on sandy lakeshores or on boats skimming over gentle waves.

Minnesota Lakes Writers write stories about Minnesota and its lakes encompassing romance, mystery, and fantasy. Our goal is to enjoy each other's love of writing and tell stories about Minnesota and its 10,000 lakes. And since there are so many, it may take us a while!

For more information, find us on our website at www.minnesotalakeswriters.blogspot.com.

ALSO AVAILABLE BY OUR AUTHORS

LANNA FARRELL

Contemporary Romance Novels:
Soldiers and Steel Capes Series
A Dark Road Home – Book One

Pride and Pack Series
Rebound – Book One

Steel Toes to Stilettos Series
Short Fuse to Happiness – Book One
Eighteen Wheels to Heaven – Book Two
Lift Me to the Sky – Book Three

Livingston Agency Series
A Grateful Heart – Book One
When Love Holds You – Book Two

The Remington Series
Matheau – Book One
Lillianna – Book Two

Dark Tribal Brotherhood Series
Brazen Rose – Book One

Anthologies:
Take Your Shirt Off and Stay Forever in *Romancing the Lakes of*
Minnesota—Spring

DIANE WIGGERT

Short Stories:
Magic at Moose Lake in *Romancing the Lakes of Minnesota—Autumn*
Love's No Joke in *Romancing the Lakes of Minnesota—Winter*
Spring Thaw in *Romancing the Lakes of Minnesota—Spring*

KRISTY JOHNSON

Short Stories:
Light Bender in *Romancing the Lakes of Minnesota—Summer*
Cara's Swim in *Romancing the Lakes of Minnesota—Autumn*
Frozen on Lake Superior in *Romancing the Lakes of Minnesota—Winter*
Fishing for Love in *Romancing the Lakes of Minnesota—Spring*

KATHLEEN NORDSTROM

Short Stories:
Break a Leg in *Romancing the Lakes of Minnesota—Summer*
The Inheritance in *Romancing the Lakes of Minnesota—Autumn*

ROSE MARIE MEUWISSEN

Contemporary Romance Novel:
Taking Chances

Short Stories:
Dancing in the Moonlight in *Love in the Land of Lakes Anthology*
Hot Summer Nights in *Romancing the Lakes of Minnesota—Summer*

Railroad Ties in *Romancing the Lakes of Minnesota—Autumn*
Blizzard of Love in *Romancing the Lakes of Minnesota—Winter*
Nor-Way to Love in *Romancing the Lakes of Minnesota—Spring*
Dance of Love in *Festivals of Love*

Children's Books:
Real Norwegians Eat Lutefisk
Real Norwegians Eat Rommegrot

PEG PIERSON

Paranormal Romance Novels:
Flirting with Fangs

Short Stories:
Fish Flirt Too in *Romancing the Lakes of Minnesota—Autumn*
A Southern Spark on Northern Ice in *Romancing the Lakes of Minnesota—Winter*
A Unicorn's Tale in *Romancing the Lakes of Minnesota—Spring*

ANN NARDONE

Short Stories:
Putting Demons to Rest in *Romancing the Lakes of Minnesota—Summer*
For the Love of Bertha in *Romancing the Lakes of Minnesota—Autumn*
Before the Trail Goes Cold in *Romancing the Lakes of Minnesota—Winter*
The Barn Find in *Romancing the Lakes of Minnesota—Spring*